# Prince of Ponies

## Stacy Gregg

HarperCollins *Children's Books*

First published in Great Britain by
HarperCollins *Children's Books* in 2019
Published in this edition in 2020
HarperCollins *Children's Books* is a division of HarperCollins*Publishers* Ltd,
HarperCollins Publishers
1 London Bridge Street
London SE1 9GF

The HarperCollins website address is
www.harpercollins.co.uk

1

ISBN 978–0–00–833234–1

Stacy Gregg asserts the moral right to be identified as the author of the work.
A CIP catalogue record for this title is available from the British Library.

Typeset by Palimpsest Book Production Limited, Falkirk, Stirlingshire Printed
and bound in England by CPI Group (UK) Ltd, Croydon, CR0 4YY

*For Brin. Really? Yes, really.*

Poland 1945

## CHAPTER 1

## *The Master of Horses*

Zofia edged her way down the ladder in total darkness, feeling her way with bare feet from step to step. She had considered turning on the lights but dismissed the notion as too dangerous. For all she knew, the Colonel was sitting at his desk right now, staring out across the courtyard. From there he would see the lights glowing in the stable block and know that she was on the move.

In the darkness, the ladder wobbled beneath her, making her stomach lurch, but she knew she must be nearly there. Only a couple more rungs and then she'd be down on ground level . . .

Made it! She felt the cold concrete floor under her feet and paused for a moment to calm her racing heartbeat. Then she continued, reaching out into the pitch black, feeling her way blindly, inching ahead with shuffling, tiny steps, until her fingertips bumped up against the wall. From here, she had her bearings and now her hands would serve as her eyes. Her fingers crept like Incy Wincy Spider along the stones until they touched the rough-hewn wood of the first door. Over the door, footsteps quickening, and then she was touching stone again, repeating the process from one door to another – one, two, three – until at last she'd reached the fourth door.

Was she certain that she had the right one or had she miscounted?

Yes – he was here! She could hear him on the other side of the door, restless and moving about.

"Shhhh," she whispered. "It's OK, I'm here now. I'm here . . ."

He didn't like being alone at night. Neither did she. They always stayed together. But tonight the Colonel had forbidden it. He'd taken her aside at dinner, his face very serious.

"It is important that you stay in the hayloft tonight," he had told her. And when she'd asked him why, he'd simply replied, "Because we have visitors coming."

*Visitors.* No explanation other than that. The way the Colonel had said the word, letting it hang in the air, was so sinister she'd known better than to ask anything more. That evening, after dinner was over and she had cleaned up the dishes after the men had eaten, she'd done as the Colonel told her and had taken herself up the frail wooden ladder that led to the hayloft.

The loft was dusty and filled with cobwebs. She never came up here in the winter and with good reason – the loft was freezing! To combat the cold, she tunnelled her way into the haystack, just as a rabbit might make a burrow, then lined her cave with burlap sacks. She moved other sacks round the edge of the skylight, pushing them up against the gaps in the timber to stop the wind whistling through. Soon, though, the wind had no way inside. The falling snow had smothered the roof in such a thick blanket it had sealed off the skylight completely. It was so deep that when Zofia tried to shove the skylight open to peer out and see where these so-called visitors had got to, the weight of the drifts was too much and the window wouldn't budge.

That had been hours ago. Midnight had ticked by and the snow kept falling and the visitors hadn't turned up. Janów Podlaski was almost inaccessible in bad

5

weather. And even in the very best weather, it baffled Zofia as to why would anyone would be coming all this way. The stud farm and the neighbouring village had no part to play in this war. They could hardly be considered a strategic location for the Germans, who currently occupied Poland. The big main cities, Warsaw and Krakow, were miles to the west, and it was a long and dangerous journey from there in the middle of winter to this tiny village in the wilderness by the Russian border. On a night like this the visitors must have realised how deadly the roads would be and changed their minds. Otherwise they would be here already.

Alone in the darkness, Zofia had mulled all of this over in her mind. She had got up and tried to prise open the skylight again to see out, but it was no use. She had looked at her watch and been maddened by how slowly the hands moved, and when the hands swept past midnight, and then began to edge towards the half-past mark, cold and lonely, she could take it no longer. The Colonel's orders made no sense! No one was coming. What was the harm then in her leaving this miserable icebox of scratchy hay and going back downstairs?

And that was how she had found herself wobbling down the ladder and feeling her way in the darkness, until she was finally at the fourth door.

"I'm here!" she breathed through the gaps in the wood as she began to work at the cast-iron bolt. "Please. Don't be angry. It was the Colonel who made me stay away from you! But now I've come . . ."

The iron bolt protested as she tried to work the door open. Zofia's delicate hands struggled to take a grip. She twisted her fingers round the nub of the shank, pulling with all her strength until finally the bolt was released with a dull thud.

She was inside the stall now, and so completely cloaked in darkness she couldn't see her own hand in front of her face, let alone the shadowy form that moved around her in the stall, fretting and stamping.

"Where are you?" she hissed. She tried to follow the sound of him as he circled her. He was moving nearer and, instinctively, she turned, thinking that she was facing him, and then realising she'd been wrong as he took her by surprise and she felt a hard shove against the small of her back.

"Hey!"

The blow pushed her off balance so that she fell

forward into the straw on the stable floor. She still couldn't see him in the dark but she felt his presence, standing above her.

"That is not funny," Zofia hissed. "I'm cold and tired and I'm not in the mood for your humour."

There was a soft nicker from the horse and Zofia immediately felt bad for snapping at him. He had only been playing! And she hadn't meant it – she'd just been caught off guard was all.

"I know." She softened her tone. "I missed you too. It's freezing in that hayloft . . ."

In the blackness that cloaked them, even without her eyes, Zofia still knew by heart every groove and sinew of his body. The way the bloom of his dapples made concentric shadows against his dove-grey coat, and his soot-black stockings perfectly defined his graceful, slender legs. Prince had just turned seven, an age when there was still a smoky darkness to his colouring. Zofia was saddened to think that the pretty dapples would fade away completely in the years to come. That was how it was with horses, and she recalled how his father had been pure white in the end. His mother, whom Prince resembled in different ways, had been a blood-red bay, and everyone had wondered what sort of foal the pairing would produce. Prince had been their first and only son, and when he was born he'd been jet black. As he'd matured into a young colt, though, his black coat had become flecked with white and he'd seemed to grow lighter by the day, so that as a yearling he was steel grey. Then the dapples emerged, and his mane became streaked with silver. In the sunshine on a clear day, when he was at liberty in the yards here at Janów Podlaski, he shone and sparkled almost like a unicorn.

"I'm here now . . ."

Her fingers reached out to touch him and traced the solid slab of his jawbone, the way his nose had that dramatic dish as it tapered to the broad sweep of his nostrils, then widened out once more, flaring like a trumpet.

His velvet muzzle sought her out now as Prince took in her scent. The soft-palate breathing as his nostrils widened, so distinctive to Arabians, made his breath in the darkness sound like the flutter of butterflies. Sweet exhalations of warm air brushed her skin, scented like clover honey. She paused for a moment there in the dark, happy to be back where she belonged, reunited with her horse.

Her happiness, like all happiness, did not last. The

soft fluttering suddenly became an agitated snort. Flashes of light outside the window startled the girl and the horse. There were headlights coming down the driveway! In the pitch black their twin beams glanced off the walls like searchlights, penetrating the bars of the stable-block windows, illuminating Prince's stall.

Zofia's heart began hammering. The visitors! They were here after all! She needed to get back to the hayloft.

She waited for the headlights to flicker past. She was just about to stand up when another set of lights came shining in through the window. A second car was arriving, and then a third.

As the car doors slammed outside, Zofia crawled across the floor of the stall on her belly until she reached the wall below the window, and then, carefully, making sure that the headlights wouldn't catch her shadow in their beam, she popped her head up just high enough so that she could see.

The three black town cars were lined up in a row in the snow. On their bonnet each car flew a tiny flag with the red, black and white symbol of the Nazi swastika. Zofia saw the symbol and felt certain now that she was in real trouble.

She should never have come down. Colonel had been clear in his orders to hidden and she'd stupidly ignored him. Now use lights had been turned on and in the driveway she could see the men getting out of their cars. They were not ordinary German soldiers either – their uniforms were not like the ones the Colonel and his men wore. These were special police, officers of the SS, dressed in black greatcoats and long boots, with red armbands emblazoned with swastikas, matching the flags on their cars.

She had to get out of here now! Run before it was too late and get back up the wooden step ladder into the ceiling then pull the ladder up behind her and close the trapdoor. Except such a sequence of actions in the cold silence of the night was not without risk. Even if she could make it up the ladder, she wouldn't have time to drag it back up into the ceiling and if the officers saw it, they'd come looking maybe, knowing someone was in the loft.

As she peered out over the window ledge one of the German officers looked in her direction and she ducked down, heart pounding, afraid she'd been seen. So now she couldn't even look at them. All she could do was crouch low and listen to their voices in the cold night air, speaking to each other in clipped German.

There were more car doors slamming, and laughter, and then she heard a voice she recognised. The Colonel. Zofia took the risk, poked her head up once more and saw him on the doorstep, wearing his full German uniform. It looked strange to see him dressed like this. In the time since the German army had taken control of Janów Podlaski, she had seldom seen the Colonel in his military clothes – he usually just wore his jodhpurs, like a civilian. And when the officers saluted him, he looked distinctly uncomfortable as he saluted back, arm raised straight out into the air: "Heil Hitler."

"Heil Hitler, Colonel," one of the SS officers replied. "I apologise for the lateness of the hour, but the snow made it impossible for us to get to you any faster."

"Of course." The Colonel nodded in agreement. "Your accommodation for the evening has been prepared and there is a meal ready. I'm sure you must be hungry. The horses can wait until morning."

"Ah," the officer replied. "Thank you, Colonel. However, such matters are not my decision . . ."

The officer turned his gaze to the second car in the row of three and at precisely that moment the driver's door swung open and yet another officer in SS uniform stepped out with great formality to open the passenger door.

The man who emerged was in a different uniform to all the rest of them. Bald, stout and not wearing a hat on his bare head, he did, however, wear epaulettes on his shoulders that clearly marked out his seniority. While his top half was very much dressed as a military man, on the lower he was dressed as a horseman in jodhpurs and long boots.

The Colonel looked anxious as he stepped forward and, uncertain whether to salute again, he tried to do so, and then changed his mind, did a half-salute and feebly offered his hand in greeting.

"Dr Rau," he said. "I am delighted. It is a great honour to have you at our stables. I was just saying to your men that perhaps you might wish to eat dinner and be shown to your rooms? It is late and . . ."

But the man did not take his hand.

"I have not come all this way to enjoy your hospitality," he said coolly. "I am here for the horses and you will take me to the stables immediately."

"Of course," the Colonel said. "As you wish, Dr Rau. They await your inspection."

*They await your inspection.* As the Colonel said these words Zofia knew she had left it too late to run. Already the flustered Colonel, accompanied by eight SS officers, had fallen into step beside the man they'd called Dr Rau, and now they were striding briskly, making their way through the knee-deep snow to the stable door. It was too late for Zofia to make it back to the hayloft. In just moments they would be here to inspect the horses and she had no escape. She was trapped in Prince's stall with no way out.

There was the sound of boots crunching on snow and then the heavy wooden doors were slid back at the entrance and the lights came on and Zofia was no longer in darkness. She could see. Which meant they could see her too. When they reached Prince's stall, there was no way they would not would find her. The stall was bare except for a thin layer of straw on the concrete floor. There was nowhere to hide.

And then she looked back at Prince. The horse was wearing a dark navy woollen stable rug. He was dressed in it to keep him warm, but right now her need was greater than his. Zofia's trembling fingers worked the front buckle and unclipped the back straps and slid the rug off Prince's back. Then, curling herself up in a ball in the furthest corner of the stall, she draped the rug over the top of her, hoping to make it look as if it had been tossed aside by a careless groom.

She hoped she'd covered herself and that no part of her body was sticking out because she didn't have time to adjust it – the men who'd been working their way along the corridor from stall to stall had reached Prince's door. She heard the bolt being slid back and then, from her hiding place, she peered out at the shiny black boots of the Nazi officers, standing right there in front of her in the straw!

"So." The voice was that of Dr Rau. "This is him, then? The one you told me about?"

The Colonel cleared his throat. "Yes, Dr Rau. This is Prince of Poland. He is purebred Polish Arabian, descended from the very best bloodlines that we possess here at Janów Podlaski. He is the finest horse in these stables."

Dr Rau gave a hollow laugh. "You are being arrogant, Colonel. You dare to tell me which is your best horse? Such decisions are mine to make and mine alone. This is why the Führer appointed me. This is why he gave me my title: Master of Horses. You understand what it means?"

"I-I meant no insult," the Colonel stammered. "I simply meant that I think him to be my best horse."

"Your best horse?" The Master turned this phrase over slowly on his tongue. "He is not *your best horse*, Colonel. He is not *your* horse at all. None of them are yours. I come here tonight on the instructions of Hitler himself. These horses belong to the Führer now. They are to play their part in his plan for the glory of the Third Reich."

"I am sorry, Dr Rau." The Colonel sounded confused. "I do not understand. I thought you were coming to inspect the stud farm. What is this plan that you speak of?"

"Ahhh." The Master almost purred with pleasure to be in possession of such top-secret information that the Colonel clearly did not know. "You are aware, Colonel, that the German army have made it part of their mission as a conquering nation to secure the very best artworks in the world? In our hands now are master-pieces by Raphael, Rubens and many more. They are works of such great beauty, the Führer demands that we ensure that they be taken by the SS and kept in secret, to ensure that when the war ends, they will belong to Germany."

"But these are horses," the Colonel objected. "They are not priceless paintings or sculptures."

"Yes," Dr Rau replied. "Horses are an even greater treasure. They are living, breathing art."

Beneath her rug in the corner, Zofia saw Dr Rau shuffle his feet in the straw and take a step closer towards Prince. He had his gloved hand on Prince's halter! Zofia's heart was pounding.

"This horse, Prince of Poland, has all the traits of the Aryan race. In time he will be pure white like his father. And his bloodlines are impeccable . . ." The Master hesitated, seemingly unsure as to whether he should unfold the whole plan to the Colonel, but was unable to resist. And so he continued.

"As we speak, my men are gathering together the very best horses in the whole of Europe – Lipizzaners from Austria, Thoroughbreds from France, and now from Poland we take these Arabians. All of them are a part of the Führer's grand scheme. For it is not just the humans, the Aryan race, who will bring glory to the Third Reich. We will also create a new super-breed of horses. The horses in your stables will be moved to Dresden. Here we will open a new stud farm, with all the best stallions and the very best mares from every breed. We will combine these horses and create the perfect, ultimate war horse."

The Colonel's voice was anxious. "You mean to say you are taking my horses?" he said. "To Dresden?"

"As I've already told you, Colonel," the Master replied, "they are no longer *your* horses, and be calm – I do not intend to take them all. Only the best stallions will serve the purpose of the Führer."

He stroked Prince's muzzle.

"You were right when you said this one is the very best horse in the stable," he said. "He is magnificent."

Underneath the rug, watching him touch her horse like that, Zofia felt a fury that made her sick to her stomach. And then the Master continued and things became so much worse.

"Prince of Poland is truly the greatest horse in your possession," the Master said. "So great, that he is not going with the others to Dresden."

"But I thought you said—" the Colonel began, but the Master cut him dead.

"In the morning, he will travel with me, back to Berlin. Hitler himself has a special plan for this horse."

The Master gave Prince a hearty slap on his neck to confirm his decision, and then he wheeled about.

"Now," he said, clapping his hands together. "I think we are done with the inspection. I should like to eat."

And with that, he marched back out of Prince's stall, with his SS officers in his wake, leaving the bewildered Colonel to bolt the door behind them.

In the darkness once more, Zofia waited until her heart stopped pounding and she was certain they had gone before she emerged from beneath the rug. She was still shaking, and as she lifted her hands up to take hold of Prince's halter, she realised just how close she had come to being discovered. At the same time, though, she knew it had been lucky that she had been in the stall to witness this, for now she knew the Master's plan.

"Did you hear what he said?" Zofia whispered to Prince. "It is worse than we ever imagined, Prince. Hitler, the Führer himself, wants you."

Prince's ears swivelled as she spoke to him. He was listening intently. Did he realise the danger they were in? Zofia knew now that there was nothing else for it and no time to waste.

"When the Master comes for you in the morning, you'll already be gone," she said to him. "You and I, we have no choice. We must run. We leave tonight."

Berlin 2019

## CHAPTER 2

# *The Hunter of Grunewald*

Mira took a tight hold of the leather leash and felt Rolf strain with all his tiny might against her control.

"Be good!" she warned the dachshund. "Or you will not get any treats."

It was a hollow threat and they both knew it. Mira was not the one to decide anything in this relationship. Rolf was in charge and Mira was his girl, hired by Frau Schmidt to do the dachshund's bidding.

At half past one, Rolf had greeted Mira, as always, at the back door of Frau Schmidt's mansion in Roseneck, and from there she and the little dog set off on his preordained Monday-afternoon outing. The first stop on their itinerary was lunch – which was where they were heading now.

Roseneck was an aristocratic neighbourhood, the pavements were broad and tree-lined, trimmed on one side with mown lawns and on the other with elegant hedges and tall fences that blocked Mira's view of the grand houses. Rolf blazed a trail through these streets with an almost comical sense of importance. Barrel-chested, pointy of snout and floppy-eared, his belly was so low to the ground beneath his long, silken coat it was almost as if he was levitating as he trotted on his stumpy legs. His lush feathered tail dusted off the concrete behind him.

Soon they reached the shops, passing the corner café where elderly ladies like Frau Schmidt would sit and chat for hours on the white leather banquettes and dine on the dainty fruit tarts displayed in the window. Beside the pretty café was another bakery; this was the one where Mira's mother worked. It was a very modern bread shop by German standards – her mother made Turkish breads here too and Syrian flatbreads along with the traditional German pumpernickel and rustic farm loaves and pretzels, all of it displayed side by side on wooden racks in the plate-glass window.

Mira looked in, hoping for a glimpse of her mother, who had left for work at 4 a.m., long before Mira woke.

There was no sign of her, so they turned the corner and pressed on past the florist's, the windows filled with pink and white long-stemmed roses, and then the Pets Deli, the first stop of their morning journey.

The Pets Deli was busy – as always. Dogs swarmed on the pavement and Mira had to duck and swerve as Rolf beetled through the throng, darting between the legs of the low-haunched German shepherds, diverting round the broad-shouldered Dobermanns in their studded collars, and barging past the bristle-coated wolfhounds to get in the door.

"Good morning, Frau Weiss," Mira greeted the woman, who was slicing venison on the machine behind the counter. "Can Rolf have his usual table, please?"

Frau Weiss grunted, "It is ready. Go on through."

Rolf did not need to be told twice. He was already heading towards the rear of the shop, where the doorway opened to reveal the courtyard restaurant.

The dachshund jumped up on to his favourite chair and Mira sat opposite him. Around them, the dogs and their owners were browsing the menu, but Rolf didn't bother. He knew what he liked and always had the same thing.

Frau Weiss was serving at the table beside them now,

fawning over a woman whose blow-dried blonde hair perfectly matched the silken coat of her Afghan hound. Frau Weiss laughed a fake, tinkling laugh as she took their order. Then she came back and, without a word to Mira, she slapped Rolf's meal down on the table in front of him.

Perhaps she never bothered to be nice to Mira because she didn't think the girl spoke good enough German? It was true that Mira sometimes got the odd word confused but she spoke it so much better than her mama, who still struggled to make the most basic of sentences. Mira had the advantage because she'd lived here since she was seven and had to speak German at school.

Now she was twelve and it was still Arabic that she spoke at home. When they'd lived in Sonnenallee, all the local kids spoke Arabic too. Sonnenallee, the Arab district, had been their home for the first five years when Mira's family had arrived in Germany. As part of the refugee programme, they had been given a place to live, a tiny one-bedroom apartment for all four of them. Her mother got a job at the cake shop on the corner of Sonnenallee and Weichselstrasse, a local hangout that specialised in Middle Eastern delicacies like pistachio slice and halva. Mira and her brother and sister went to school during the day and in the afternoons they ran loose with the other kids of the neighbourhood, playing football in the park on the corner of Reuterstrasse, dangling from the climbing frame, until it was too dark to see and they were forced to go home.

Six months ago, they'd moved to Roseneck to be near her mother's new job. Her mother had said that Mira would get used to the neighbourhood but Mira still hated it here. Her mother had always worked hard before but now it was like she didn't exist. She'd already left for work by the time Mira woke up in the morning and she was never home until after Mira had put her brother and sister to bed at night and was asleep too. The rent cost more here, Mira's mother said, and working long hours was the only way to make a better life. But Mira wanted to know why they couldn't just go back to their old life in Syria. Or at the very least back to Sonnenallee, where she had friends.

In the corner of the dog café, Mira sat at the table and watched Rolf as he polished off his luncheon, relishing each bite with a little growl of delight. He ate in stages, licking the gravy off the liver and veal first, then moving on to the main dish before toothily devouring the bigger chunks of chopped-up blood sausage. Finally his pink tongue circled the dog bowl to get the very last bits and then, licking his chops, he looked up at Mira.

"Ready to go, *habibi*?" She smiled at him. "Come on!"

Out on the street, Rolf immediately began straining at the leash. His tummy was full and he was keen for his morning walk. And for once they had perfect timing. The bus was waiting for them at the corner.

Mira took Rolf in her arms and jumped on board. They sat like that, her cradling the dog in a seat near the front. It wasn't a long ride. Only three stops from the shops to reach the gates that led into the forest of the Grunewald.

A paved avenue swept from the street into the car park, and from there the path turned to sandy loam and began forking off in all directions through the conifers and the birch trees. Today they were taking their usual route, which led all the way to the Grunewaldsee lake. It was going to get hot and Rolf might fancy a dip.

Once they were on the sand paths, Mira bent down and unclipped Rolf's leash to let him loose. As soon as he was free, Rolf shot off, sprinting away and then scampering in a ragged half-circle before running straight back towards her, his little legs churning like mad, his pink tongue lolling out to one side. Mira laughed at him. It was always the same, this moment of over-excitement. Soon he'd calm down and trot along with her companionably. But first he needed to burn off some energy.

Mira watched the little dog as he bolted ahead of her to do his second sprint-and-circle-back, running at breakneck speed round the curve of the path until he was out of sight. She strode on briskly after him, expecting that when she turned the corner she would see Rolf there, panting and exhausted, heading back towards her on the path ahead. But when she came round the corner, there was nothing. The wide path that cut through the forest was empty. Rolf was nowhere to be seen.

"Rolf!" Mira called out. "Rolfie?"

She whistled for him. And then, with more urgency in her voice, she called again, "Rolf!"

The sound of yelping broke the silence of the forest.

Rolf! His bark was echoing through the trees to the east of the path and he was going bonkers! Had he caught scent of something? A squirrel, perhaps? Rolf lost all common sense when he was confronted with a whiff of prey. And these woods were big. If he got away from her, it would be all too easy to lose a little dog like him!

Mira began dashing through the trees, following the dachshund's caterwaul. Rolf's barking had now become one long, persistent hunting yowl, which meant he must have that squirrel trapped up a tree. Were squirrels fierce? What if Rolf got into a fight with it and it bit him? Frau Schmidt would blame Mira if the little dog should come to any harm.

Mira's heart was pounding as she came into a clearing in the woods and saw Rolf. He was pronging up and down furiously on the spot, all stiff-legged and wild-eyed as he bailed up his prey. Her relief at finding the dachshund was immediately replaced by shock at the size of his adversary. Because it wasn't a squirrel that Rolf held captive at all.

It was a horse.

The miniscule dog stood bristling and barking furiously, while right in front of him a white stallion, barricaded in by the pedestrian turnstiles and rails of the rustic fence that ran beside the forest path, was stamping and fretting, turning back and forth in his futile attempts to evade his tiny foe.

Their eyes were locked on each other in the same way that a matador engages a bull in battle. This fight, however, seemed to be rather more one-sided. The horse had to weigh at least six hundred kilos more than Rolf, and he towered over the dog as he manoeuvred back and forth in front of him. Despite the difference in size, the stallion seemed genuinely scared of the dachshund. Mira could see the fear in him, the way his dark eyes turned wide and his nostrils flared and snorted with each tempestuous breath.

With his neck arched and tail held high he was so beautiful he appeared almost otherworldly. At first sight he had struck Mira as alabaster white, but now she saw the faintest bloom of dark dapples on his rump, and the darkness of his mane and tail, which were burnished steel.

The stallion kept trying to outmanoeuvre the dog, pivoting on his hocks, turning and trotting back and forth, and then reversing abruptly, trying to double-back and duck past. It seemed ridiculous that he could be kept prisoner by Rolf. And yet here they were, locked in an impasse.

Rolf, for his part, had failed to notice that the horse was a hundred times his size. Determined to hold his prey, he kept blocking the horse at every turn and making little darting leaps, threatening to bite if the stallion stepped out of line. If the horse stepped too far forward, Rolf would snarl and lunge to push him back. And whenever the stallion tried to go sideways and break into his magnificent floating trot, Rolf would sprint forward and dash to head him off, forcing the horse to skid on his hocks to a stop, pinning him to the fence once more.

Mira watched as the little dog lunged and snapped, and this time the horse got fed up with this game of cat and mouse with his captor and fought back. The stallion lunged right at Rolf! He had his ears flattened back against his head, teeth bared, neck winding and twisting like an angry snake. He struck out and got so close to biting the dog that Rolf retreated for a split second. But then the fearless dachshund redoubled his efforts, barking and snapping. This war between them was escalating! Mira watched as the stallion went back on its haunches, striking out with a front hoof that narrowly missed cracking Rolf on the skull!

"Rolf! No! Get back!"

Rolf was oblivious to how much danger he was in, but Mira could see that one blow of those hooves could bring about his death.

As the horse rose up to strike out again, Mira found herself running forward to grab the dachshund. But Rolf didn't want to be saved. He swerved away from Mira, evading her grasp, and she had no choice but to throw her body down on the dirt to get a hold of him.

"Rolf!" Rolling in the dust, Mira clung to his collar and pulled him roughly to her. "You must stop this! He will kill you!"

The horse was now directly above Mira and Rolf. With a startled snort, he went up on his hind legs, striking out violently with both front hooves. Mira let out a shriek and shut her eyes, certain the horse was about to come down on top of them and trample them. But somehow the stallion planted his hooves on either side of her and then he went up again and this time he spun on his hocks, turning away to face the fence that had him trapped.

There was no space to jump but the stallion was undeterred. From a standstill, he gathered himself, rocking back on his hindquarters, and then he popped in one tight stride and stag-leapt, effortlessly clearing the rustic rail with daylight to spare.

Mira couldn't believe it. The horse hadn't even needed a run-up. He had just launched himself into the air, as if he had springs beneath his hooves! And the way he landed on the other side was as graceful as a cat. As soon as he touched the earth, he sprang away at a gallop and, with a defiant shake of his mane, he set off towards the other side of the woods, weaving between the birches and conifers so that he became a grey blur between the trees.

Rolf was beside himself: his quarry was getting away! He began baying again and, in a last-ditch effort, he managed to squirm and rip himself free from Mira's hands.

"Rolf! No!"

This time the dachshund only managed a few short strides before the leather went taut at his throat. Mira, anticipating that he would try to escape again, had already clipped the leash to his collar when she'd tackled him to the ground, and had slipped the loop at the other end round her wrist. Rolf only got to the end of the leash before he was yanked back again.

"Let him go!" Mira admonished him. "What were

you thinking? You cannot possibly catch a horse! And what would you do with him if you did catch him? You are crazy!"

Rolf wasn't listening, though. He was still wild-eyed and hyped up, giving hysterical whimpers and gazing longingly into the trees, even though the horse, having galloped away at lightning speed, was gone from sight.

Mira reeled Rolf back, inching along the length of the leash until she had him in her hands once more.

"Where did he come from?" she asked the dachshund. But she was asking herself more than Rolf. It was not unusual to see horses in the woods, but they were always taken out by riders from the riding school. Horses didn't turn up in the middle of the forest running wild all on their own!

Rolf, twisting and squirming in Mira's arms, demanded to be put down and she lowered him back, still keeping a tight hold on the leash.

The little dog shook himself with indignation and then he dropped his head to the ground and began to sniff in earnest.

"Rolf," Mira cautioned him. "No. Leave it. We need to go home." She knew what he was doing. Dachshunds like Rolf were renowned for their skill as tracking dogs.

Mira had read in a book once that an olfactory trail could be left to go stale for as much as a month and a dachshund would still be able to nose out a scent that was strong enough to hunt by. To Rolf, the smell of the white stallion was fresh in his nostrils and it was irresistible.

"Rolf, ugh . . . no. This way! The bus stop is this way . . ."

Mira tried to distract him from the scent trail and turn for home. But Rolf took to whining piteously and refusing to budge, and whenever she tried to pick him up to carry him he darted between her legs.

"Rolf!"

Mira sighed. "You're so stubborn," she told him. And then she smiled to herself, because it was something her mother often said to her as well. They were alike, she and Rolf. And, right now, it seemed they both wanted the same thing. Because the truth was, Mira wanted to find the horse too.

"You think you could do it?" she asked the little dog. It seemed unlikely in a forest this size and yet Rolf seemed so set on it, so determined to give chase.

"OK, then, *habibi*, darling one. You can do it. Go. Find him."

Mira kept the leash round her wrist and held on tight. Rolf took up the trail with a yelp and was once again on the hunt, and this time Mira did not resist. This time he was taking her with him.

## CHAPTER 3

## *The Emir*

Rolf was so intent and focused as he sniffed it was as if he held the whole universe right there in the tip of his nose. The scent trail of the horse was so strong to him that the path ahead might as well have been illuminated with fairy lights.

Mira felt his certainty as she was dragged down steep slopes where the leaves had fallen so thick that she was buried to her knees. She slid down, over mossy logs and rotting tree trunks, then found herself clambering and crawling back up again. They were deeper into the heart of the forest now and had left behind the broad, sandy avenues where they usually walked.

*We should go back. We'll get lost and no one will ever find us* . . . Mira was thinking this when Rolf stopped in his tracks, and the leash in her hand went slack.

They were here.

They were standing on the ridge of a hill looking down through the trees to a clearing below. To the right was the pitched shingle roof of a small house, with what looked like a barn attached to it. In front of the buildings, two large yards for exercising horses, with a sandy loam surface, were enclosed by posts and rails.

Rolf cocked his head and let out a whimper as the doors to the stables opened. From inside Mira could hear the echo of horses' hooves on the cobblestones, then a loud blowing snort and a moment later the grey stallion appeared through the doorway. He came out and as soon as his hooves touched the sand he broke into a high-stepping trot, his strides so elevated and bouncy it was almost as if he floated above the ground. He carried himself in a taut composition of muscle and sinew, his neck arched and his eyes on the woods beyond, his tail held erect so that the silken plumes of it trailed out behind him like gossamer as he circled the yard. He swept along right beside the rails as if he were looking for an escape route, and Mira noticed as he did this that the fence round the yard had been altered. The whole yard had been painted with dark brown fence stain, but there was a newly added unpainted rail that had been roughly hammered on at the top of the fence, which added another half a metre at least to the height of the barrier.

The stallion did two laps of the enclosure, and then, with a sudden prop, he slammed on his brakes, making the sand come flying up from beneath his hooves. He came to a dead stop, pivoted on his hocks so that now he was facing the opposite direction, and broke into a gallop. As he raced across the yard making for the rails, Mira really thought he was going to jump. She was reminded of the effortless way he'd popped in a single stride to vault the fence in the forest. But this fence now was almost twice that size. Mira watched as the stallion came up on to his haunches and then, reconsidering, he dropped down again with a jolt and drove his front legs deep into the sand to stop himself, ploughing a channel as he skidded and crashed into the rails, pivoting on his hocks to turn, bouncing away in frustration, then circling round the fence, snaking his neck and tossing his mane in consternation.

Then he halted, sides heaving like bellows, and looked up at the ridge where Mira and Rolf were watching.

His ears pricked forward. He'd seen them! From the yard, he raised his elegant head and gave a clarion call, whinnying out to them.

Mira hesitated for a moment and then she gave the leash a yank. "Come on," she said to Rolf. "We're going down there."

They scrambled down the bank together, a tangle of limbs and dog leash, until they reached the bottom, both of them panting, with hearts pounding. Mira picked Rolf up and felt his little feet waggling in mid-air as he tried to jump down again. She didn't want him to scare the horse, so it was better perhaps if she went alone from here. She took Rolf's leash and tied the dachshund to the fence. The stallion was standing perfectly still watching them, his dark eyes wide and calm.

Rolf growled a little, as if he were cautioning Mira when she stepped away from him and circled the fence to move closer to the horse.

She climbed up the rails and the horse stepped closer to her. Then he craned his elegant neck so that his muzzle was only a metre or two away from Mira's face. She reached an arm out to him. The horse didn't shy away from her, but stepped in again, stretching his muzzle to her hand. Mira wished she had a treat to offer him instead of her empty palm.

The horse stepped closer again and now he was standing almost side-on to her. All she needed to do to get on to his back at that moment was to stand up on the fence rail and turn sideways a little and make the leap. If she did so, she would find herself sitting on the horse's back!

Behind her, she could hear Rolf give a low warning growl, but she didn't turn to see what the dachshund was grumbling about. Her total focus was locked on the horse that stood there in front of her. She stood up, wobbling a little as she found her balance, perched on the rail on the balls of her feet, her hands still clinging on to the top rail. Her heart was pounding as she shimmied herself along the rail a tiny step or two, so that now she was in the perfect position just next to the horse's broad, silver-grey back.

As she leapt, two things happened at once. The first was that the horse did not stay still as she'd expected him to do. Instead, he gave a startled snort at the sight of the girl propelling herself through the air, and he bolted. The second, more remarkable thing, was that Mira found herself suspended in mid-air and then abruptly jerked backwards again, so that when the horse disappeared out from under her, she didn't fall to the ground. She had been grabbed from behind and now she found herself not falling but being held in strong arms and eased down gently to the earth.

And then, in her ear, louder than the sound of her own heart pounding, came the staccato bark of a woman chastising her in furious German. Mira turned round to see that the person who'd taken hold of her was an old woman, and the lady was yelling at her in rapid-fire language, speaking so quickly that Mira couldn't possibly hope to keep up with the words.

It was hard to believe that this frail, elderly figure in front of her had been the one who'd just pulled her back from her daredevil leap. And yet that seemed to be the case as she was now standing there, arms waving wildly as she gave Mira a piece of her mind!

The old woman was dressed in an ancient flowery silk blouse tucked into faded green tracksuit trousers. She had brown knitted woollen slippers on her feet and her fine white hair was swept up into a loose bun that was twisted and pinned with a wooden clasp at the back. She was still barking away in German but it had at least slowed down from the rapid-fire shouting to a mild yelling. Mira tried to understand her, listening hard to decipher what was being said. Something about a king? No, not a king exactly. An emir! And then the penny dropped and Mira realised: that was his name! The horse – his name was Emir, and the woman was talking about him.

"What did you think you were dealing with here? Some tame riding school pony?" she was asking. "Emir is sensitive, powerful, highly strung. You are lucky that he did not kill you! If I had not got to you in time, this would have ended very badly for you."

"I'm sorry," Mira muttered.

"You should be!" the woman snapped. "Now clear off! Get out of here. This is private property, you know. Not the public forest. If you want a riding school, there is one in Grunewald near the Waldsee. Go there instead!"

"I . . ." Mira was too terrified to respond.

"Go on! What are you still here for?" the woman barked. "Are you simple-minded? I told you to leave!"

"I need . . . to untie Rolf," Mira replied. She pointed over the woman's shoulder to the little dachshund, who was still hitched up to the fence post. Rolf, seemingly unaware of the tension between Mira and the old lady, was standing up on his hind legs rather adorably and, at the sound of his name, he began yipping and wagging his great plume of a tail.

His foolish antics made the old woman lose a little of her bluster. "Yes, well," she harrumphed in a gentler tone. "Of course. Fetch your dog and go."

"He's not my dog," Mira said.

"What?" the old woman growled.

"Rolf is not mine," Mira said. "I take care of him for Frau Schmidt. I'm not allowed a dog of my own."

"Why on earth not?" The old woman frowned.

"A dog is another mouth to feed." Mira was repeating her mother's words, the phrase she used whenever Mira had asked for a pet.

"Who cannot afford to feed a mouth this small?" the old woman scoffed. "Typical, though, I suppose. People always think of themselves first, never of the animals who suffer . . ." Tutting and muttering away, she bent down and patted Rolf. The dachshund, oozing charm now, stood up on his hind legs to meet her and all the anger in the old woman disappeared and she gave a little laugh.

"Do you know, I had a dog like him when I was your age. Well, not really like him. Olaf was a Polish hound, much bigger than a dachshund, but he was a good dog.

And he was so loyal, just like lovely little Rolf here . . ."
She looked as if she were about to continue the story,
but her eyes turned misty and she trailed off and turned
back to Mira instead.

"Your German. It is strange. You speak with an
accent. Where are you from?"

"Aleppo," Mira replied.

"Aleppo?" the old woman grunted. "Where is that?"

"Syria."

"A refugee, are you? I'm sure they do not have horses
where you are from, so you know nothing and think
that you can come along like that and just throw yourself on to his back?"

"We have horses," Mira objected. "And I know how
to ride. I rode in Syria. There was a stable in the city.
I went every week on a Wednesday."

"Well, that makes it even worse! You should know
better than to try to mount a strange horse like that!"
the old woman shot back. "And just because you rode
some donkey back in the desert, don't think that makes
you a rider."

"It wasn't a donkey, they were good horses," Mira
insisted. "I do know how to ride. I had proper lessons."

The old woman screwed up her face. "Perhaps you

have ridden a little. But nothing you have ridden in the past could have prepared you for him." She gave a whistle and the stallion, who had been standing at a distance on the far side of the arena, pricked his ears and stepped obediently towards her. The old woman waited for him to get closer and then she waved one hand in the air above her head and made a clucking sound with her tongue. Suddenly the stallion rocked back on his hocks and pivoted round so that he was facing the far side of the arena and in one swift powerful bound he accelerated forward and leapt up into a trot. His head and his tail were both held high and his front hooves seemed to flick out in front of him, as if he were dancing across the sand.

"Do you see that trot?" The old woman watched him proudly. "So expressive, the way he covers the ground. He is an amazing mover and the power of his paces is far too much for all except the very best of riders. If you had managed to climb on to his back, he would have put you on the floor in an instant. You are not prepared for a horse like Emir."

Mira watched, entranced by the movement of the horse. "He must be valuable."

"He is priceless," the old woman replied. "His bloodlines are the very best in the world. An Arabian from Poland – like me."

"You're Arabian?"

This made the old woman chuckle. "I'm Polish, child. And you are Syrian. So it seems the only one of us here who is a true German is Rolf."

She cocked an eyebrow at Mira.

"You speak German very well for a refugee. Tell me, can you write it too?"

"Yes," Mira said. "Yes, at school they say my writing is very good."

"Then," the old woman said, "you had better come inside. We will have some tea, I think. I've baked some angel wings, and you may have some if you like? Do you like sweets? Bring the dog. He will want some too."

And without turning to look back to see if Mira was following her, she set off across the yard towards the door to her house, shuffling in her slippers, with Rolf bounding at her heels.

\*\*\*

The house was divided from the stables by an archway. Turn one way and there were three looseboxes and a hay barn, turn the other and you were almost immediately inside the old lady's living room. This was where Mira found herself now, staring at a room that was decorated with needlepoint tapestries all over the walls. It was furnished with old wooden furniture and armchairs that seemed to be covered in a floral print similar to the old woman's shirt, so that when she'd made the tea and put the angel wing biscuits on the table and sat down, she almost disappeared into the upholstery.

"Do you read?" she asked Mira as she passed her the plate of biscuits and tossed one on to the floor for Rolf.

"Yes," Mira said. "I love books." And she realised as she said the words that this was what was bothering her when she looked around the room. There were bookshelves on the far wall but they were covered in ornaments. No books. She couldn't see a single book in the whole house. Mira didn't have many books of her own. She mostly read what she could from the school library, but she did have a few copies on her little bookshelf in her room, and she loved them. They were her most prized possessions.

"Hmmm." The old lady seemed pleased with the reply. "Reading is good. I should like to be able to do it myself. But I can't." She looked at Mira. "Oh, yes, I tried! And I went to a very good school, so my education wasn't lacking. My parents expected that I should be clever. My father was a professor and my mother had been a teacher. All my uncles and cousins were very intellectual, but . . . for me . . . it was never possible. From the very beginning, the words bounced around on the page and would not behave. My mother couldn't understand it, because she had always read to me. We had a library full of books! They decided I must be stupid. I wasn't, of course. It was dyslexia. These days people know all about it. It is a condition that means you get the letters jumbled up in your eyes and your brain and to decipher them becomes impossible. But back then, no one knew this. And so I was just the half-witted girl who couldn't read. And I guess that was what they always thought of me . . ."

The old woman trailed off and dabbed at her eyes with a handkerchief that she took from her sleeve. "Anyway. It is not reading I wish to do. It is writing."

She put the handkerchief down and threw Rolf another angel wing, although she did not offer another biscuit to Mira.

"I am dying," she said.

Mira looked shocked, until the old woman added, "We are all dying, of course, but I am old, very old – I'm eighty-nine, if you can believe it, so I am closer to death than you. One day I will die from old age, and it might not be that long. And before I do, I have a story – one that I would like to see recorded so that it might be told. It is important, I think. I lived in remarkable times."

She reached out to Mira with the plate of biscuits now, but Mira noticed how she held it back a little, as if the offer of the biscuit itself was contingent on what happened next.

"You will write for me," the old woman said. "I will tell you my story and you will put it down in words on paper."

"And why would I do that?" Mira asked.

"Because," the old woman replied, "I will be making you an exchange. If you will write my story for me, then I will do something for you."

"What?" Mira asked.

The old woman took a biscuit herself now and mashed it between her gums and followed it with a vigorous slurp of tea.

"I'll teach you to be a horsewoman," she said. "And

if you are a good student and you mind what I say, then, yes, I'll let you ride Emir."

Mira couldn't believe what she was hearing.

"What do you say, then?" the old woman asked.

Mira leant forward and very slowly and deliberately she took an angel wing from the plate.

"Excellent!" The old woman smiled and Mira saw just how gappy her grin was and how much work it must have been to chew that biscuit. "We shall start tomorrow. You will come back to my house. Bring the little dog with you if you like."

"I have school tomorrow," Mira said.

"Well, come before school, then," the old woman replied, as if this solution were obvious. "I wake early."

"OK," Mira agreed.

The old woman stood up and made it clear that, with the arrangements sorted, their afternoon tea was now over. As they walked to the door, she made a fuss of Rolf and gave him one last angel wing. "For being a good boy," she told him, with a pat. Then she opened the door for Mira. "I will see you tomorrow, child," she said.

Then, almost as an afterthought, she called after her:

"You haven't told me your name. What do they call you?"

"I'm Mira," Mira replied.

"It is a pleasure to meet you, Mira," the old woman said. "My name is Zofia."

## CHAPTER 4

## *The Devil and the Sea*

My name is Zofia. And as I told you yesterday, I am Polish. I was born in a forest village, Janów Podlaski, to the east, miles from the excitement of the big cities of Krakow and Warsaw.

Don't worry, Mira. I promise I will not bore you with the dull, happy days of my early childhood. I don't want you to fall asleep when you should be writing! I will skip the first nine years of my life because nothing of importance happened, and I will begin this memoir on the date my whole life changed forever: 1 September 1939. The day when Adolf Hitler sent his Nazis to invade us and take over Poland. That was the start of the Second World War, of course, although we did not know it then. Within days of Hitler crossing our border, the French and the British declared war and after that . . . Hey! Mira, are you keeping up with me?

***

Mira, who had been frantically scribbling away as Zofia spoke, was suddenly shaken back to reality and the tiny living room where she was sitting once more with Zofia, Rolf, a pot of tea and a freshly baked batch of angel wings.

"Yes, I am keeping up," Mira lied. She had such cramp in her hand from trying to write the old woman's words and – look! They had only completed one page!

Zofia was suspicious. "It's important that you stop me if you are being left behind, because I want to make sure you are getting all my words down correctly. This is actual history I'm telling you. After I die, who will know the truth about these events except me? This is a record of what happened and I don't want any of it to be lost, so from here I will go slower for you . . ."

Rolf, who was sitting on Zofia's lap, gave a theatrical yawn at this moment and Mira noticed how his little pink tongue unfurled and snapped back again behind his sharp teeth. Zofia chuckled at the antics of the little dog as he stood up and stretched and resettled himself, then she drank a sip from her teacup and resumed her story once more, speaking every bit as fast as before, so that Mira had to scribble frantically to keep pace.

*** 

Hitler was such a bully! And a liar! Do you know he said we started it? Can you believe that? He claimed that he was only invading Poland because we had attacked first, but of course it wasn't true. The Nazis struck without warning, sending troops from the north, the south and the west. We weren't prepared, and none of our allies came to help us. As the Germans advanced closer and closer to our village, my parents decided we had no choice but to abandon our home and flee to safety.

I remember my mother being very firm with me when we left the house. I wanted to take all my toys but she'd said that I could take only one, a brown knitted squirrel named Ernst. I carried him myself in my tapestry carpet bag, along with a change of clothes. My mother and father carried everything else. Because I had my hands free, I was entrusted with taking care of Olaf. He was our family dog, a strapping great hunting hound, not at all like our little Rolfie here. And there was me, just a skinny nine-year-old, trying to hang on to him. It took all my strength to keep him from pulling away from me on the leash when we set off, but after we had left the village behind and we were on the open road my father said I could safely let Olaf off the leash and, sure enough, he trotted along obediently, staying close to me.

On the road, our ranks swelled and other villagers joined us, all heading towards the river. The River Bug marked the border into Romania, and if we could make it across the bridge, then we'd be out of Poland and away from the German danger.

We walked alongside all these other families, hundreds of us making our way to the river. I know it sounds awful to say, but I remember that day as a rather exciting one. There was a sense of adventure about it all. We were all banded together on this journey, and that night the families gathered round an open fire, and we grilled sausages and cooked potatoes in the embers and there was singing. My father had a *koza* with him – you have probably never seen one and the closest thing I can compare it to is a Scottish bagpipe. My father played it well. He was an academic, a professor of Polish studies, and in Janów Podlaski he was very respected as a member of the *Gmina* – the district council. Often he would have meetings at our house. As I said, he was very well educated and my mother was too, so I think this made it even harder for them that I couldn't learn to read or write.

Anyway, I am straying away from the story. My father played the *koza* that night and we sang. There were couples dancing and we were all singing along and it was only after the embers in the fire had died away to nothing that I went to sleep.

In the morning, we rose early and began walking again, the mood uplifted by the night before. There was talk on the road that day about the river, how it was not far now. We were almost at the border and the sides of the road were dense with forest.

As the day passed by, bands of travellers who were moving faster than we were would catch us up from time to time and our ranks would swell briefly. Sometimes they'd stay with our group, but other times they were too quick to keep our pace and they would leave us behind and disappear into the distance. So I knew that there were people on the road ahead of us, I suppose. All the same, it came as a total shock when, at the end of that second day, in the late afternoon, when we still had miles ahead of us to cover, we saw them all coming back towards us.

It was everyone that had passed us by, and a few others besides! They were heading back with as much urgency as we were going forward! As soon as we saw the looks on their faces, we knew things were very bad. My father ran forward to meet the group, and his face when he returned to us – it was very grave.

"We're going back," he said. "We must turn at once for home."

"But that is crazy, Pavel!" My mother was stunned. "For all we know, the Nazis have already arrived in Janów Podlaski. We can't go back!"

"We can't go forward either," my father replied. "Magda, look up ahead! Do you see the smoke?"

Now that my father said this, we could all see smoke billowing on the horizon. "The Red Army have bombed the village of Kovol," my father said. "They're coming, Magda. They're on the road, and they are heading straight for us."

"The Russians?" My mother was horrified. "How close?'

"They march nearer the longer we hesitate," my father said. "We must turn and go home."

If the mood on the road up until this point had been

59

one of buoyed spirits and camaraderie, now it could be summed up in one word: fear. We were on a road in the middle of nowhere, unarmed, defenceless and trapped between two unstoppable armies. Instead of running from Janów Podlaski, we were now heading home and back into the clutches of Adolf Hitler.

"Mama?" I asked anxiously. "Will the Nazis be there? Will they treat us better than the Russians?"

My mother managed to summon a thin-lipped smile and she took my hand in hers and squeezed it tight. "They can hardly be worse!" she said.

"Why do they want Poland?" I asked.

"Hitler is flexing his muscles and expanding his empire," Mama replied. "He wants more *Lebensraum*: living space for the German race."

Mama stroked my hair with her hand. "The Germans come to rule us, but there is no reason to believe that they will harm us."

Later, when things had turned truly bad for my family, I would think about what my mama said to me that day and wonder if she knew the true evil of Hitler's vision and was keeping it from me because she didn't want to scare me. In this new world, Hitler would rule Poland, the Germans would occupy it and the Polish people would be their slaves. But then, slavery was not even the worst that Hitler had in store for us.

***

We'd been on the road heading back for home for several hours when we heard a sound ahead, rumbling through the forest. As the rumble grew nearer, the earth beneath us trembled as if there was thunder under our feet. My friend Agata, who was walking nearby with her parents, and who until now had been very quiet, suddenly burst into floods of tears.

"It's the Germans!" she sobbed. "They are coming for us!"

It wasn't just Agata – others were crying too, and as the thunder grew closer, people began running in all directions.

"We must escape into the trees!" Mama cried.

"No!" my father said. "It is too late now. They will shoot us if we try and run from them. Stay behind me. I will wave the white flag and they will know that we are unarmed."

My father had his white pocket handkerchief in his hand, ready to wave as he stepped to the front of the cavalcade to face the Nazis. I felt my whole body shaking now as the thunder grew and grew, until at last they came into view.

I have never in my life seen such a sight as I saw that day.

What came at us round the bend in the road wasn't the Nazis at all. It was horses – almost a hundred of them. Wild and loose, running together as a herd, so many of them jammed on the road that they were pressed up shoulder to shoulder. It was the pounding of their hooves, overwhelming in unison, that shook the ground under us!

Flanking this wild herd, mounted on horseback, were a dozen men. Each of them carried a rope and a whip, and they were attempting to keep the horses moving forward together, which was not easy. They might as well have been trying to herd cats! The most difficult were the young ones, tiny foals who ran, bewildered, at their mother's side, flagging with exhaustion. Then there were the yearling colts and fillies, who kept breaking loose so that the men on horseback had to ride out in wide loops to bring them back to the herd again. Every time they rode out to rescue one of the colts who had bolted away, they would lose control of the rest of the group, and then there would be even more horses to muster back before they got lost in the trees.

Until this moment, the only horses I had known were the thick-set, plodding creatures who pulled the carts in our village. These horses were totally different. They were all fire and glory, and they almost floated above the ground, their paces were so smooth and balletic. It was as if, with each stride, they were held suspended in mid-air. I was mesmerised by their gracefulness.

Seeing that the horses were about to collide with our party, one of the men on horseback began shouting out orders to his men, and they rode swiftly forward to bring their own horses in front of the stampeding ones, turning about-face to create a blockade. Confronted with the men on horseback, the wild herd came to a standstill. Just like that, a hundred wild horses were brought to a halt, corralled right there in front of us on the road.

"Pavel?" The man who had given the orders now turned to us. He'd recognised my father and my father knew him too.

"Vaclav." My father shook his hand. "It is good to see you, my friend."

"Why are you turning back?" Vaclav asked.

"The Russians," my father explained. "They're advancing. For all we know, they're already at the river."

Vaclav shook his head ruefully. "So we are stuck between the devil and the deep blue sea. If we turn back, the Nazis will certainly seize our horses."

"Yes, but, sir," one of his men shot back at him, "if we encounter the Russians, it will be worse! They will eat them!"

As the men were debating what to do, I was admiring the horses. There was one particular colt that caught my attention. He was dark steel-grey, with sooty black stockings that ran up all four of his legs and a white snip on his muzzle. He was so beautiful! It wasn't just his looks that captivated me, though – it was the way he carried himself. He moved constantly, fretting and stomping, as if he had hot coals beneath his hooves. With his neck arched and his tail aloft, he pawed and pirouetted, flicking his noble head up and down in consternation. I remember that day – how all the other horses seemed to melt away, and at that moment there was only that grey colt right there in front of me.

One of the men on horseback, a young groom, noticed me staring at the colt.

"He's beautiful, yes?" he said.

"Yes." I nodded. "He's my favourite."

"You have a good eye!" the young groom said. "The Janów Estate breeds the best Arabians in the whole of Europe. And Prince is without a doubt the very finest of them all. He's worth a lot of money."

"Is that his name? I asked. "Prince?"

"Prince of Poland is his full name," the young groom corrected me. And then he untied a rope from his saddle and handed it to me. "Put this on him if you want, and you can lead him back. He's quite the escape artist this one – always bolting off away from the herd. It would help us if you led him on the journey back, since it appears we are now going home again."

"Really?" I asked.

"Sure," the groom said. He tied the rope to the shank of the colt's halter and then he passed the end to me. I took hold of it, like I was grasping the tail of a snake.

The young groom laughed at me. "No. You must get in close. Hold the colt tight, right up at the shank of the rope. You are safer being close to him – he cannot take a hoof to you if you are right beside him."

"A hoof?" I squeaked.

The young groom nodded. "Prince is pretty handy with his front hooves. I was leading him back to the stables the other day and he rose up on his hindquarters and struck me across the back of the head. Knocked me out." He saw the look of fear on my face. "He was just playing. He's spirited, that's all – not a bad horse, just a hothead. You can do this. Just keep your eyes on him and stay at his shoulder and move with him whenever he moves. Yes, there! You're doing much better already. You see how you can use your body to block him and keep him in line? That's it . . ."

Looking back, it was crazy to give me such an unpredictable horse to handle. I was only nine! But it certainly took my mind off the Russians. I had my eyes glued to Prince as he danced and fretted. I should have been afraid, I suppose, with all the talk of deadly flying hooves and this half-wild horse dancing wildly at my side. But there was so much else to fear that day that the horse slipped down the list of things that I needed to be afraid of. And, after a while, it seemed to me to be second nature to have him bouncing and prancing along beside me.

That groom needn't have bothered to tell me to watch Prince, because at that moment I couldn't take my eyes off him. He was so beautiful the way his sinew and muscle rippled beneath grey steel. The black stockings that marked his elegant ballerina legs, and the gossamer silver of his silken mane. The proportions of his face were so perfect they were almost unreal, from the deep curve of his concave profile to the taper and flare of his sooty velvet muzzle. And his ears. He had such small, delicate ears, curved in a little and short and sharp. They swivelled about to catch my words as I spoke to him. This horse was smart, and he was listening intently to everything I said. Horses do not talk, of course, but they are good listeners.

As we walked down the road that day, with the sun setting, I talked and talked with Prince beside me, his ears swivelling the whole time. I told him all about my life and my family. I knew nothing of his own family at that point, of course. It was only later that I would find out that Prince's own parents, like mine, were here on the road with us. In fact, Prince's sire, his father, was that impressive, powerful white stallion the head groom himself was riding. Prince's mother was with us too, running with the mares. She was a dark bay with limpid brown eyes. I wish I'd realised who they were, because I would so have liked to have gazed at them, just that once. After this day was over, I would never get the chance again.

We were on the road and I was just thinking it must almost be time to set up camp for the night, when the planes came. There was the roar of engines and then the black shapes silhouetted in the sky above the trees. Three aircraft, coming from the south-west. There could be no doubt that they were German Luftwaffe, the airborne attacking force, and a moment after they came into sight, the planes directly opened fire!

There was screaming and suddenly everyone was running everywhere. The horses were completely forgotten – all anyone cared about was getting to cover as the planes flew closer and closer, all the while firing on us relentlessly. I saw a horse fall in a hail of machinegun fire, and at that moment I knew this was all too real.

"Don't they see we aren't soldiers?" my father was shouting. "There are women and children here!"

Bu the Germans didn't seem to care. They were firing at us.

I wish I could say that I held my nerve enough to keep hold of Prince, but that would not be true. What happened next was not because I held him. It was my own nervous habit that bound us together. As we'd been walking, I'd been fiddling with the rope, looping it round my wrist.

I didn't realise how dangerous this could be or that, the instant the gunfire began and Prince startled and bolted, the rope would jerk into a tight knot and I would be literally dragged off my feet and into the forest behind the runaway colt.

I remember being flung about on the ground as if I were a sack of hay, and then the roughness of the bracken against my skin as Prince dragged me off the road and into the trees. And then I must have hit something with my head, because when I woke up, everything was woozy and I felt a lump on my skull almost as big as my fist, throbbing and hot from where I'd been struck. Prince, all heaving and sweaty, was still there, standing over me. And the rope was tight as a hangman's noose round my wrist, so my fingers had turned white from lack of blood. When I wrenched off the rope, they tingled for ages with pins and needles, and there were rope burns and bruises. That rope saved me, though, because Prince had managed to wrap it round a tree when he'd bolted. The rope had pulled taut and had tethered him tight to the tree trunk, so in the end he can't have dragged me very far. He'd tried to break free, but no matter how hard he pulled on that rope, it had only tightened more round the trunk and bound him to the tree. So the rope held him, and it held me. I had to cut myself loose with a pocketknife, but I left Prince tethered to the tree until I could figure out what to do.

I was still woozy. The last thing I remembered before I was knocked out was the machinegun rattle and the sky filled with German planes roaring above. Now the noise was gone. The sky was silent. And the forest too. And when I shouted out for my parents, again and again, there was nothing. Everybody had gone and we were alone . . .

\*\*\*

Zofia rose to her feet, forcing little Rolf to stand up and leap off her lap on to the carpet. "We will finish now," she said.

"No!" Mira was distraught. "We can't stop now. I need to know what happens next!"

"It will have to wait until next time," Zofia said, pointing at the clock above the fireplace. "Mira, you are late for school."

## CHAPTER 5

# *The Lesson*

The bus was running so slow that day! Mira sat in her seat with Rolf in her arms, feeling more and more anxious. By the time she'd handed over the dachshund to Frau Schmidt and run the two blocks down the street from there to her school, she was almost a full hour late for class.

"You need your teacher to sign your late slip," the secretary at the office told her. Mira filled in the slip. She wrote her name and the date and then, under "Reason for lateness", she scribbled the first thing that came into her head.

"What is this that you have written here?" her teacher, Herr Weren, asked her when she offered him the note as she entered the class.

Herr Weren read from the late slip out loud to the class: "Reason for lateness: Hitler invading Poland."

He turned to Mira. "That is not funny, Mira."

"I'm not trying to be funny, Herr Weren," Mira said.

"Well, you are very successful, then!" Herr Weren said curtly. "Perhaps you had better stay behind in detention when everyone else goes to morning tea today and make up for wasting all of this time."

"Yes, Herr Weren," Mira said.

When the bell rang, Mira stayed in her seat. Herr Weren took out a newspaper, kicking his chair back and putting his feet up on the desk.

"Am I allowed to have my morning tea?" Mira asked.

Herr Weren looked up from his newspaper and raised an eyebrow. "Under the rules of the Geneva Convention, I believe you have the right to eat," he said. Then he gave a chuckle at his own joke, which Mira didn't understand. But she figured that he meant yes, she could, and so she unpacked her lunchbox from her bag. There was some hummus and carrots and a heavy brown German kind of bread that Mira didn't like much at all, which her mother brought home from the bakery.

The clock on the classroom wall ticked very loudly.

Herr Weren looked up at it wearily, already bored with disciplining his pupil. He put down his newspaper. "I think that's enough," he said. "You can go out and play now, Mira."

"Do I have to?" Mira said.

"What?" Herr Weren was confused. "Yes, Mira, I'm letting you go now."

"Oh." Mira's voice was heavy with disappointment. The truth was, she'd been delighted to get a detention and she was less than thrilled that it was now over.

Herr Weren walked to the door and held it open for her. Mira stuffed her lunchbox back in her bag and slung it over her back. Herr Weren stood waiting. She was moving so slowly, this child!

"Is there something wrong, Mira?" he asked.

"No, Herr Weren," Mira said.

"Come on, then! Off you go."

Outside in the playground the other kids had already eaten lunch. The boys were mostly on the field playing football. The girls' activities, on the other hand, were much more divided. There was a big group of girls playing Fang on the field, and there were more playing netball on the courts. Mira hurried past them. There was a place, just at the end, where she usually sat at break times. No one else went there, and all she had to do was wait and hope that no one came by before the bell rang. Today, though, when she rounded the corner, there were already three girls there. They were playing a game they called elastics. Two of the girls, Hannah and Gisela, stood with knotted pairs of tights stretched like bands round their legs. They stood with their legs braced wide, so that the tights made a taut loop round them, and the third girl, whose name was Leni, had her back to Mira and was jumping back and forth, scissoring her legs across the tights as the other girls chanted a rhyme:

> *"Jingle jangle*
> *Silver bangle*
> *Inside – out – on!"*

Leni was taller than the other two girls, so she had the advantage in this game because of her longer legs. She was wearing blue shorts and a white T-shirt and her ice-blonde hair was cropped in a very short bob, rather boyish in style; the other two girls were both much mousier, with long hair in ponytails.

"Hey!" Hannah caught sight of Mira before the others. "Look, Leni, it's Cockroach."

Leni stopped jumping. She turned round and smiled at Mira. It was a smile that made Mira feel sick. She knew what was coming.

"Cockroach!" Leni greeted her. "Have you come to play with us?"

"No," Mira said, shaking her head, backing away a little, slowly, the way you might back away if you had suddenly stepped into viper's nest and you were trying to get out again without being struck.

"Come on, Cockroach!" Leni said. "We want to play with you."

The other two girls had taken the tights off their legs now. They circled round behind Mira and took the tights in their hands and stretched them taut between them, so that now, as Mira backed away from Leni, she found herself pressed up against the tights. She bent down and ducked to get past, but the girls, giggling, lowered the knotted tights so that this didn't work, and Mira was trapped. Leni, meanwhile, kept advancing.

"We thought we weren't going to be able to play with you today," Leni said. "It's a good thing Herr Weren let you out, huh? Now we can play after all."

"I . . ." Mira could feel her heart racing. "I don't want to play."

Leni ignored this. "You shouldn't be at this school, Cockroach," she said. "You should go back to your own country."

Mira could hear her voice inside her head. And her voice, it was shouting: *You think I don't want to go back? I hate you! I don't want to be here at your stupid school!*

But no words came out of her mouth. She'd tried to fight back against Leni before and it had done no good. She'd ignored her and stayed silent, and that had been bad too. Either way, it was bad, and Mira knew it was coming.

This time, though, it wasn't Leni who struck first. There was a hard shove against her back. Mira didn't know if it was Gisela or Hannah who'd pushed her; they were both laughing as she stumbled forward and they were on top of her before she could regain her balance, pushing her face-first to the ground. She felt them grab her wrists. And then they had her arms all the way behind her back, wrenched so hard that it felt like her shoulders would be pulled from their sockets, and the tights, the ones the girls had been playing with a moment ago, were being wrapped round and round her wrists, binding her hands together behind her back.

Mira felt the grit of the playground pressing against her stomach and then, when her hands were bound tight, the girls flipped her over on to her back.

"On your back, squirming with your legs in the air like a proper cockroach!" Leni said. That smile still hadn't left her face. That smile was often the last thing Mira would see when she turned out the lights at night before she went to sleep. That smile terrified her.

Leni leant down over Mira's face now, drink bottle poised. "I'm going to drown you, cockroach."

She held Mira's nose as she poured the water all over her mouth. Mira tried to shut her mouth to stop the water going in but then she couldn't breathe, so she had to open it again. The water flowed in but she couldn't get the air down at the same time and she was heaving and choking. She couldn't breathe and she could hear Hannah's voice, sounding anxious: "Leni, you should stop now. She's choking. Leni?"

And Leni's voice in reply: "Going to drown the Cockroach. Cockroaches shouldn't be here. Cockroaches need to die."

And then the water in the bottle was all gone and Mira was coughing and spluttering and there was the sound of laughing and the school bell ringing to signal that playtime was over.

***

Mira knocked nervously on the door and heard the footsteps coming, then the sound of the chain being put on before Frau Schmidt slid open the door a crack, just enough to see who was there.

"Mira?" Frau Schmidt was taken aback. "I wasn't expecting you."

"I thought perhaps Rolf might like some exercise?" Mira offered. "He had such fun in the forest the other morning, and I know he loves an outing. I have time this afternoon to take him to the Grunewald again, so I came here to see if he wanted to go for a walk . . ." Mira saw the hesitation in Frau Schmidt's face.

"Free of charge," she added.

Frau Schmidt seemed pleased by the offer now. She slid back the chain and undid it, opening the door wide. Rolf, who had been standing at her ankles all this time, immediately bolted outside and ran circles round Mira.

"I think he is keen." Frau Schmidt smiled.

***

Mira needed Rolf. She didn't want to admit it, but she was smart enough to know it was true. Zofia had tolerated Mira yesterday, but she had seemed to adore the little dachshund. If Mira was to turn up this afternoon for her riding lesson without the dog, Zofia would be devastated. No. Rolf was necessary, like the sweet layer of sugar that her mother used to coat the doughnuts at the bakery. And from now on, as long as Mira was having riding lessons, Rolf would be getting a free afternoon walk.

"This is good for both of us," she whispered to the tiny hound as they approached Zofia's house. "So behave yourself."

Rolf looked up at Mira with shining black gooseberry eyes, his pink tongue hanging out to one side. He was quite exhausted already from the walk here. Hopefully he would spend the next hour while Mira was riding lying flat-out asleep on the stable floor.

*While she was riding.* Mira ran that sentence through her head again, played it back and forth. She liked how it sounded. Back home in Syria, her family had not been rich, but things had certainly been very different to how they were now. There was money for things – things like riding lessons. Mira hadn't been lying when she'd told Zofia she'd ridden before. But perhaps, looking back, those horses at the riding school her father had taken her to, they had been – what did Zofia call them? Plodders! Mira's heart was racing as they got closer to Zofia's.

"Hurry up, *habibi* darling!" This time it was Mira dragging Rolf in her haste to get there!

Emir was in the exercise yard when she arrived. He was at liberty, trotting around with his neck craned towards the top rail of the fence. He looked, as always, as if he had plans to leap the rails, despite the fact that they were taller than he was. He trotted defiantly, his nose in the air, and when he caught sight of Mira and Rolf he began showing off, upping his trot to a canter, circling the yard and shaking out his mane and throwing out his front legs, striking at the air as if to say, "This place won't hold me for long."

Mira watched the way he moved, the way his reflexes were so acute he could change direction in a heartbeat, flinging himself back on his hocks and pirouetting in mid-stride to face the opposite direction. The explosive power of his paces enabled him to move from a high-stepping trot to a flat gallop without missing a beat.

"He is very special, isn't he? My Emir is no ordinary horse."

It was Zofia. The old woman was still in her knitted slippers and floral blouse as she shuffled her way towards Mira across the yard.

"You see how he extends naturally like that?" Zofia gestured at the stallion as he floated back once more into a trot and began to flick his front legs out, lengthening his strides so that he glided across the arena and made it from one side to the other, barely touching the sand. "He's got the paces of a purebred – expressive and magnificent. You shouldn't be learning how to ride on a horse like this. A beginner like you should be mounted up on a nice, slow pony. A gentle little slug that will potter about and be kind and sweet. Emir is not these things. He is challenging, even for the most established, the most experienced rider. It is not that he is disobedient – he is very well schooled. But he is physically gifted in ways that are not easy to control. When you are on his back, his movement is going to be so big, so powerful, you will find it impossible to stay on. Your balance, your co-ordination, is not ready for such a horse. Yesterday, when you climbed the fence to throw yourself on his back, if you had managed to get on him, he would have killed you."

She saw the disbelief on Mira's face.

"I am not joking. He could kill you. To ride Emir is to ride a rocket ship. And you are not yet ready to be an astronaut."

"But you said I could have a lesson," Mira said.

After the day she had been through, to turn up here now and have the old woman admit she wasn't keeping her bargain was almost too much to take.

"I'm giving you a lesson," Zofia said. "But it will not be on Emir."

The old woman bent down and picked up Rolf. "Come on," she said to Mira. "Come inside the stables. Your mount is waiting for you."

\*\*\*

There were three stalls inside the stables. Zofia walked past the one that had the gold plate on the door with the word "Emir" written on it. She carried on to the next stall, which she unbolted so that Mira could follow her inside.

In the stall, right in the middle, were three hay bales stacked on top of each other. The top hay bale had a saddle girthed round it and in front of the stack was a rake strapped to the bales. From the prongs of the rake a bridle had been draped.

"What's this?" Mira was confused.

"This," Zofia said, "is your horse."

"I don't understand," Mira replied. "It's just hay."

Zofia ignored her and walked over to the bales. "But let us pretend it is a horse. It is the same size and almost the same shape. It has a saddle and bridle. So come here and show me: if it were a real horse, how you would mount up?"

Mira wanted to just say no. This was stupid. But maybe if she just humoured the old woman? Maybe then she would let her on Emir? She walked over to the saddle and put her hands on it and began to clamber up.

"What in Saint Adalbert's name are you doing, child?"

"Ummm, getting on my horse?"

"Is that how they taught you to do it in Syria?"

"Ummm, I don't know. I didn't pay attention. We just got on them," Mira said.

"Did you just?" Zofia rolled her eyes. "Well, with horses, there is a right way and a wrong way to do everything. Including mounting up. If you had tried to scramble up Emir like that, I can tell you you'd definitely be dead by now. A horse like him will not stand there and let you climb up as if he's a climbing frame! Now do it again and this time properly. Here! You begin by standing alongside. No – the other way! You face the tail, yes, that's right, like that. And then you take the reins and gather them into your left hand. Now you reach to hold the pommel – that is the front of the saddle – with the same hand. And then you put your left foot into the stirrup and your right hand on the back of the saddle – the cantle – and spring on your right foot. One-two-three – and swing the leg over the back of the horse so that now you are on board."

Mira had her foot in the stirrup already as Zofia said this, and now she twisted her torso and bounced, one-two-three, and leapt and swung her leg. And there she was, landing light as a feather in the saddle. She felt rather pleased with herself until Zofia said, "Well, that was clumsy! The way you swung your leg over the hay – if that had been Emir, you would most likely have kicked him in the backside! So once again you are dead. Get down and try again. No. Don't clamber down! We are back to square one, I can see that. Now I'm going to have to teach you how to dismount from a horse too."

It was bad enough that Mira didn't get to ride a real horse that day, but she barely even got to ride the hay horse. The hour swept past with Zofia giving her instructions on how to get on and get off again, how to hold the reins, and how to sit in the perfect position with a line between the horse's bit and her elbow and another line running down through her body: shoulder, hip, ankle. It was only at the very end that Zofia showed her how to balance up in her stirrups and then lower herself back down into the saddle so that she was "posting", the movement she would need to perfect so that she could rise to the trot.

The clock on the wall said the hour was over long ago and they were almost at the end of the lesson when Mira tried to rise up to the trot. Suddenly the hay shifted underneath her, wobbling to one side. Mira shrieked in surprise and Zofia leapt on her in a fury.

"No squealing! You are on a horse!" she snapped at Mira. "This is not fun and games. This is serious."

She looked at Mira and shook her head. "You may dismount now. In the correct manner that I showed you earlier, please: reins in the left hand, drop the stirrups, swing the leg . . . try and land like a cat and bend your knees as you do so, or it will hurt when you hit the ground. Better than last time, but you are still so clumsy . . ."

Zofia's mood did not improve as she showed Mira how to untack her horse, naming all the parts of the saddle and bridle, showing her how to unfasten the straps, and where to stand as she did so.

All this time, Rolf had been asleep in the corner of the stall. Now he came to rejoin them, looking deeply bored and yawning so that his pink tongue unfurled.

"You did better at the end," Zofia said. "I think tomorrow we will be ready to ride."

"On Emir?" Mira felt her heart leap.

Zofia gave a sceptical laugh. "My goodness no, child! We are still far from that point. But at least you are no longer behaving like a sack of potatoes up there. So tomorrow afternoon perhaps I can actually put you through your paces. Until now, you were unteachable!"

And with that Zofia gave up on Mira entirely and focused all her attention on Rolf, scratching the little dog behind the ears and bending down so that her face hovered above his snouty muzzle. "As for you, my dear boy, I will see you tomorrow of course too! I am baking a fresh batch of angel wings for you especially."

Mira didn't ask if there would be angel wings for her as well. On the whole she thought not, as Zofia didn't say anything more as she showed Mira and the dog out of the door.

## CHAPTER 6

## *The Red Army*

There was a lump the size of a golf ball on my head. And as well as the rope burns on my wrist, there were scratches down my arms and legs from being dragged along when I'd stumbled, fallen and hit my head. I am guessing this, as I couldn't really remember any of it. Nothing beyond the moment when the planes began firing at us.

The noise of the gunfire had terrified me. Now what scared me more was the silence. There was no sound at all, and no one in the woods, it seemed, apart from me and the colt.

"Mama! Papa!" All I could hear was the sound of my own voice echoing back at me through the trees. Surely if my mother and father were anywhere near, they would be calling for me too? How much time had passed while I was unconscious? It was dark now, so perhaps it had been hours.

It was as I strained to listen for my parents that I heard the noises. There was something moving far off in the woods on the distant hills. It could have been the horses – so many had got loose and scattered when the planes were firing on us. Or it might be wolves. The forests here were known as their hunting ground, and it was night-time now – they would be awake and looking for prey.

I did not know which way I was going myself until that moment. I had looked at the dense forest in all directions and realised I did not know which way the road was or how to get back to Janów Podlaski, but now I knew that, no matter what, we needed to be going in the opposite direction to whatever it was in the woods that was making the noise.

I began to lead Prince through the trees, but as the undergrowth became more dense I found myself getting tangled in branches and unable to push my way through and hold on to Prince at the same time. That was when it occurred to me that it would be faster if I was riding him. It was possibly the most ridiculous thought I had ever had, but out there in the forest in the middle of the night, it seemed a rather sensible solution. If I was on his back, we could move easily, as one, through the trees. And so I decided to climb on to him. Except that didn't prove to be as easy as I expected. I tried to vault up off the ground, but that was futile. He was too tall for me to leap up unaided. And so I looked around for something to give me enough height to jump from.

"Prince." I tried to coax him over towards a fallen tree so that I could clamber up. "Good boy, come to me . . ."

But of course he didn't! He was not yet two, and had never had a man on his back! No wonder he would not stand still for me. I tried turning him round again and again, climbing back and forth on the log and preparing to throw myself on to him, but every single time I got myself into position ready to leap, he would skitter away from me again, snorting and shaking his mane as if to say, "No way!"

And then there was a moment when I managed to get Prince to stand still, and as he planted his feet square beside the log, I was already in position and from there it all just happened in a blur. I leapt into the air and then suddenly, incredibly, there I was: I was on his back!

You cannot imagine the triumph, the sense of wonder at being astride for the first time. It was this inconceivable.

To be on a horse was something I had dreamt of all my life, and now here I was. I was riding!

This feeling lasted approximately two seconds, before Prince gave a startled grunt of objection and catapulted me promptly through the air with a buck that was so swift it sent me flying in an arc to hit the ground like a beaten lump of lead.

I struggled up, lunging to grab at his dangling lead rope before he could escape, and managed to get it just in time.

My heart was hammering in my chest from the shock of the fall. Adrenalin was coursing through me, making me ignore the pain in my ribs from where he had flung me to the ground. And then I looked at poor Prince and I realised the terrified colt was even more shaken than I was. He had not expected me to do that to him, and now he reeled away from me at the end of the lead rope, the whites of his eyes showing in the darkness.

"Oh, Prince, I'm so sorry," I tried to calm him. "It's all going to be OK. I would never hurt you. Only we need to do this. I need to get on your back. You can trust me. Come on, now."

It was hard to be calm, to try and do things slowly, gently to soothe him. Because inside, inside I was hysterical with fear myself. I had realised now that the noise in the distance was not wolves – I could hear voices, distant but quite clear on the night air. They spoke a language I knew but didn't understand. They spoke Russian.

I remembered the look on my father's face when he had returned to us with the news that the Russians were coming and how scared everyone in the cavalcade had been as the word spread of the advancing Red Army. Vaclav's grooms had said the Russians would eat the horses. And now here I was in the forest, and in the distance I could hear noises in the hills. The sound of the Russian army advancing towards me.

I don't know how I convinced Prince to put his faith in me that night. Maybe he knew, as I did at that moment, that we no longer had any choice: we had to band together if we wanted to live.

Steadying my nerves, I pulled at Prince's lead rope once more, encouraging the colt to step back towards the fallen tree. "Easy, boy." I spoke softly to him, stroking his neck. "There's nothing to be afraid of."

I was lying. There was very much a reason to be afraid. The Russians were coming. And I needed this to work now or both of us would be dead. But for the sake of my horse that day, I tried to stay calm and I took deep breaths into my belly. As I did this, I heard Prince breathing too, blowing out through his wide nostrils. *Stay calm*, I told myself, and I felt my heartbeat slow. Still speaking softly to him, I stepped closer. To begin with, I put one arm out, reaching gently across his back, and then, once that arm was resting on him, I moved the second arm across, just as gently, making no sudden movements. And then I tilted my body forward and rested my torso against the colt, so that the weight of my arms and chest lay flat across him. When I lifted my feet off the log so that all my weight was on his back, there was a split second when I felt him tense his muscles, as if preparing for the buck. But this time it didn't come. And I was lying there across the colt, like a sack of potatoes being taken to market. I probably didn't weigh much more than a sack of potatoes, to be honest – I was only nine and as skinny as a sparrow. All the same, this was new for both of us.

I remember I lay there like that for what felt like an eternity. Possibly it was not much more than a minute, but all the time I could hear the voices, and I knew that they were on the move in our direction and getting nearer, and all the time I had to resist my urge to rush things. I couldn't afford to be bucked off a second time. Waiting was the most painful thing in the world, and today, whenever I am training a horse or a rider and I have the urge to push too fast too soon, I always say to myself, "Zofia, take your time, you have plenty of it. It is not as if the Red Army are advancing on you!" So that day, when the Russians were in the woods so close I could smell their cigarettes on the air, I steeled my nerves and took my time, and I did the impossible – which is nothing. I lay there, perfectly still, allowing the colt to get used to my presence. And then, there was the moment when I felt what I needed to feel: the sensation of the colt letting his breath out, a soft blowing snort exhaled through his wide Arab nostrils. I knew then that he was ready, and at that point I swung my leg over his back, gently, and I sat up slowly once more.

This time, he didn't try to buck me off. But then again, we hadn't yet tried to move! And I had no idea how to make a horse go forward. Still, I'd learnt my lesson from that first fling through mid-air, so this time I didn't make any sudden, strong movements. In the forest that night I developed the methods as a rider and trainer that remain with me to this day. Never do more when you are riding than you need to do to achieve your goal. Never kick when a gentle tap or squeeze should be enough. If the horse is relaxed and in tune with you, as he should be, then your cues need only be quiet. And we needed to be quiet at that moment because the Russians, having stopped to regroup, were now advancing on us at a steady pace. I could hear them marching towards us – the forest was alive with the sound of them so near to us.

"Come on," I breathed softly to Prince, "we should go now. There are men behind us and it's not safe here."

I did not mention the horse-eaters to Prince. I didn't want him to be as afraid as I was. I just closed my legs a little on his sides and almost cried with relief when he walked for me.

We walked through the woods that night, the darkness cloaking us. Riding bareback is slippery, and I kept sliding this way and that as I struggled to get my balance on Prince's back, having to adjust my seat as the colt manoeuvred his way between the trees. At times a branch would suddenly loom in front of me, a black shadow coming out of nowhere in the darkness, and I'd have to be swift to flatten down low on Prince's neck to avoid being swept off his back. Once, when a bough sneaked up on me too quickly, my only escape was to collapse backwards so that my head lay on his rump! All of this was good training for the colt, who was getting comfortable with the notion of a rider moving on his back. And for me too, the bareback skills I learnt as we navigated through the woods at night were making me develop a stability that would become so ingrained in me that one day I'd be able to show jump a Grand Prix round bareback better than I could with a saddle. But of course we did not think of what we were doing that night as "training". All we were doing was trying to stay one step ahead of the Red Army. Trying to stay alive.

I was discovering my balance all the time in the darkness, and when at one point we reached a steep hill with a clear dirt path that wound between the trees, I tried trotting for the first time. I took a hank of mane and wrapped my hands in it for grip and then I tightened my legs a little more and Prince seemed to know what I was asking and began to trot – which was very bumpy – and then, luckily for me, the trot became a canter, which was smooth and powerful. I slid back a little, but I managed to hold on and not fall, and in those moments, as Prince surged up the hillside, we put enough distance between ourselves and the Russians to feel a little safe for the first time that night.

When we emerged from the woods at last and reached the road once more, the moon was full and I could see that we were going in the right direction, and that, incredibly, we were on the road that would lead us home. I was so relieved that I wept a little.

I never did see the Red Army soldiers who'd been in the woods right behind us that night, although at one point the footsteps and voices had been so close I think if it had been daylight they would have seen us. And I have no doubt that if they had found us, we would have been murdered. So without the colt, I would have died, and without me, he would have died too. It was knowing that I owed my life to him that made the events that followed take shape in the way they did. I would have given anything for Prince from that point onward. And despite knowing that the Nazis were probably ahead waiting for us, it was with a sense of triumph two days later that I rode my horse back into Janów Podlaski, back to my home town once more.

***

My house was still there and, from the outside, it looked just as we had left it when we'd fled. There was even a pile of half-chopped wood on the front steps that my father had been in the process of stacking when we made the decision to go.

Right beside the house was the chicken coop and, a little further along, the sty where our pig, Liga, lived. The chicken coop would be too small to hold Prince, but the yard of the pig sty would be big enough to keep him enclosed while I went and found my parents inside. Liga was no longer living there. We had let her loose when we fled, figuring she would do well enough foraging for herself in the woods.

"Mama?" I yelled as I ran to the house.

"Mama? Papa?"

The front door was wide open – the lock had been smashed.

"Mama?" I stood on the doorstep, too scared to go inside, afraid of what waited for me there.

And then, in the shadow beyond the door, I saw the outline of the body on the floor.

The body was lying there motionless and it took me a moment to recognise who it was.

"Olaf!"

My dog didn't raise his head. I felt sick, thinking the worst, as I ran to him and threw myself down to the floor at his side.

"Olaf?" He was covered in blood. There was a gaping gash above his eye where he had been struck by something very hard. My poor, brave dog! I saw it all now. The Nazis had been here. They'd come into our house, Olaf had fought them and he'd leapt at the Germans to come to my parents' defence. But a dog's loyal love is no match for the crack of a soldier's rifle butt across the skull.

"Olaf!" I hugged him tight, the tears choking in my chest. And then, as I held him, I heard him give a whimper. He was still alive! The blow to the head must have knocked him out cold, but he was not dead.

Later, I would think back to how lucky it was that the Nazis had knocked him out like that. If he hadn't been rendered unconscious, then Olaf would have kept fighting and he would have been shot for sure. As it was, the Nazis had left him for dead, assuming the blow to his skull had been fatal.

We sat for a while longer as Olaf regained consciousness, and then I fetched him a bowl of water and he lapped it up gratefully. I left him to recover while I searched the house. As I entered each room I feared what I would find. But there was no one there.

There was nothing to eat either. When we'd fled the house, we'd taken all of our food. It had been two days now since I'd last eaten and I was light-headed with hunger.

"Olaf." I coaxed the hound to his feet. "We have to get out of here – they may return."

My dog followed me outside to the pig sty, and I climbed up on to the stone wall to mount Prince.

I wasn't sure where to go. I considered riding into the village, but if the Nazis were here now, surely that was where they would be?

Then I thought of the stud farm. It wasn't far from here – maybe a half-hour's ride. I had nowhere else to go, so what else could I do? After all he had been through, Prince was going right back to where he started from.

\*\*\*

The entrance to Janów Estate was a bridge across a river, and the gates were very grand, set into a stone wall with castle turrets on either side, and one of the turrets had a sentry box attached.

There was no guard in the box and the gates were open. I rode Prince straight down the driveway, towards the elegant white buildings up ahead and the arched entrance of the stables themselves.

When the stables were in sight, Prince raised his head and gave a whinny. It was a clarion call, a cry to say he was home, and it was answered immediately by another horse. So we were not the only ones here!

We rode in through the arch, and then further down the driveway, with the house on one side and the stables with the cobbled yards. Beyond the stables were the turnout paddocks. And there right in front of us they were all there – fields full of them! The horses I had first seen galloping towards me on the road to the River Bug. They were grazing happily, just as they had done before their adventure. One of them, a chestnut mare – perhaps the one that had called to us before – stood with her eyes trained on us and gave us another whinny. Prince returned her call, and I felt him shaking as he cried out, sensing the incredible joy and relief in him to be here and to be home. I felt myself choking back tears, because at least he had his family back, even if I did not yet have mine.

And then behind me there were voices and the front door of the house opened and a man stepped outside.

I had been expecting Vaclav. But this man was not him. His manner of dress was unmistakable: a grey uniform with jodhpurs and long boots, and a gun holstered at his hip. As he walked towards me, Olaf gave a low rumbling growl.

"Don't come any closer," I said. "My dog bites."

"Your dog," the man replied, "looks as if he has been in a fight already and come off the worst."

"He's not scared of Nazis," I said.

"Is that so? And how about you?" the man asked.

"I'm not afraid either," I shot back.

"Really?" The man looked at me and his thin lips did not smile.

"Let me tell you now . . . that you should be."

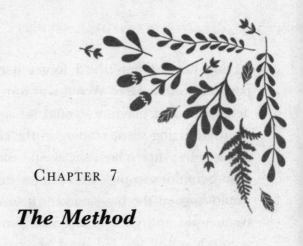

CHAPTER 7

# *The Method*

For a week now, Mira had turned up every morning at Zofia's house and written down the old woman's memories. Sometimes, by the time she got to school, she was unable to close her fingers on her pen because her hand was cramping so badly. Zofia still spoke so quickly! There were moments too when Mira would find herself so transfixed by the story she would forget to write. And then Zofia would look at her and say something gruff like, "Am I wasting my breath, Mira? I am very old and there is not much of it left." And Mira would be shaken back to her senses and hurry once more to scribble everything down.

The routine was set. At school she tried very hard to stay out of trouble, but at best she would settle for staying alive. Often she'd forget her homework on purpose so that Herr Weren was forced to give her a detention, and playtimes could be spent in delicious seclusion doing silent reading in the classroom, where it was safe. After school she would run all the way to Frau Schmidt's to pick up Rolf for his walk and they would hop on the bus and return to the gates of the Grunewald and walk to Zofia's again and she would write while Rolf was fed angel wings and if she finished the text to Zofia's satisfaction then there would be a riding lesson.

Was it really a riding lesson, though? She was beginning to think the old lady was a fraud. Mira would straddle the hay bales while Zofia shuffled about with Rolf in her arms, cooing over the dachshund while she ran Mira through what she referred to as her "Method".

It began with the warm-ups. While Zofia busied herself with putting china cups on the tea tray and bringing it out to the stables, Mira would be working through the routine. She would mount the hay bales in exactly the way Zofia had shown her and then dismount again. She did this a dozen times, over and over, and then the rising began. As Zofia chanted, "One-two, one-two," Mira would stand up on the balls of her feet in the stirrup irons, put her hands on her head and then sit again. Zofia always complained that she was doing it wrong.

"Heels deep and knees relaxed. Always light with your seat," Zofia would say as Mira came back into the saddle. "Your back should be like a ramrod, but instead you are flopping around like you have jelly for bones. Come on, keep the eyes up! Look between his ears!"

"There are no ears!" Mira would argue. Her horse's head was nothing more than a bridle that had been strung on the top of a rake propped up in the hay bale in front of her.

Zofia had taken ages to get the rake at just the right angle, clucking and tutting to herself as she adjusted it and the bridle until it suited her. When Mira complained very vigorously at one lesson that the rake in no way resembled a real horse, she turned up the next day at her lesson to find that Zofia had painted googly eyes and nostrils on the garden implement to solve the problem. Mostly, though, she ignored Mira's complaints outright, and would block them by chuckling or chatting away to Rolf as if Mira couldn't hear what she said. "That girl of yours has too many opinions, my little friend. She needs to listen. Too much to say for herself . . ." And Rolf would cock an ear and look at Zofia, as if he was in total agreement with the little old lady, for which he would be rewarded with an angel wing.

Sometimes, while these "riding lessons" were going on, Emir would be right there! He'd be in one of the stalls, tucking away happily on a hay net. Other times he would be at liberty in the sand arena and, once she had been put through the Method for the day, Mira would always pause for a few minutes to watch him before she made the walk home through the woods with Rolf. Emir seemed to relish having an audience and as soon as he saw Mira sitting on the fence rails he would begin his performance. Sniffing at the ground with wide nostrils, he'd begin blowing and snorting and hanging his head low at first, so that his nose was almost trailing the ground as he trotted along. Then, suddenly, he would raise it up high to look over the railings, changing his stride to a high-stepping trot, elevating his legs, before flowing into a powerful, expressive canter as he looped the arena and skidded to a halt, throwing up sand beneath his hooves, before looping back in the opposite direction. Although Zofia had never talked about what happened the day that Mira and Rolf found Emir in the forest, Mira always assumed that the newly tacked-on rails that now made the fence almost two metres high in some places had been put in because the stallion had jumped out. And sometimes, when he put on a sudden spurt of speed and charged at the rails, she thought that, even with the super-high fences, he was thinking he might try it again.

Watching Emir flinging out his front legs in play and giving little snorts of excitement, Mira would feel a desperate urge to be on his back and find herself despairing that it might never happen at all. By now she'd written almost fifty pages, narrow-spaced, of Zofia's story, telling how she had escaped for Romania only to be forced home again. The old woman made her work so hard in their sessions that Mira's hands would be cramping. Some days that she could not grasp Rolf's leash on the walk home. And yet they seemed to be no closer to Zofia's promise of teaching her how to ride the Arab stallion.

Today, when Mira entered the stables, it was the same as always. There were the hay bales set up and waiting for her, and Zofia instantly leapt upon little Rolf and fussed happily over him. The dachshund was getting so fat from all the angel wings that his belly now scraped the floor, and Frau Schmidt had commented to Mira that, considering the fact that dog was being walked twice a day, it was hard to fathom why he was gaining so much weight.

"You may begin the exercises," Zofia said as she left the stables to make tea and left Mira doing her usual routine, mounting and dismounting, over and over, and rising up and down with her hands on top of her head. When Zofia ambled back in her knitted slippers, with Rolf bounding alongside her, Mira could see that she had made two cups today, prepared in colourful fine bone china on a silver tray.

Zofia set the tray down on a table next to the hay bales and watched as Mira finished off the last of her rises in the stirrups. Thinking she was done, Mira was about to dismount from the hay when Zofia grunted to indicate they were not yet finished, and handed Mira the silver tray. "Do it again and hold the tray at the same time. Hands nice and high."

"But I'll spill it," Mira said.

"I don't see why," Zofia said flatly. "You should be able to rise up and down with a tray of tea in your hands without slopping a drop. A rider's hands must be independent of their seat. Now hold your hands closer together, and keep them up in the air as a pair. Tray in your hand and thumbs on top. Loose, relaxed arms. You see, you must keep it straight, a perfect line from the elbow to the bit."

Mira took the tray and sat down in the saddle. When she stood up again, the tea in the yellow cup with the roses on the saucer slopped over the edge a little.

Zofia tutted. "You need to focus harder, Mira. Keep your hands steady, child. Use your lower leg for balance."

Mira tried again. This time the tea wobbled in the cup as she rose up in her stirrups and sat again, but it didn't spill.

"Better," Zofia said. "Except that you are moving too slowly. Up and down, keep a rhythm, go on my count: one-two, one-two . . ."

Up and down Mira rose in time to Zofia's count and on the third time she sat down, the tea sloshed. Mira tried to adjust the tray as it wobbled, but her efforts only put her further off balance and she lurched forward, so that this time the white cup with the blue and lilac periwinkles disgorged half its contents on to the plate.

Zofia took the teacup from the tray and emptied the saucer, pouring the tea back in the cup, and replaced it.

"Try again," she said. "And this time, when you rise up, I want you to tilt your body at the hip and lean forward and stretch the tray out in front of you, as if you were offering the tea at a distance to someone very grand, and bowing graciously to them at the same time."

Mira looked at the old woman in disbelief and plonked the tray of tea down. "But I didn't come here to learn to serve tea to grand ladies! I want to learn to ride a horse and you make me do all this – all this . . . nonsense! And still you do not even let me near him!" Mira began scratching at her legs. "Look at me! I have a rash from sitting on the stupid hay bales! This is not horse riding! This is crazy. You are crazy!"

Zofia looked at Mira and then at the tea tray. "You've just spilt some again," she said. "I'll fix the cup and we can start again."

Mira didn't know how she managed to get through the session that day. So many times, she wanted to walk out and just tell Zofia she was never coming back. But then she thought better of it. She had a plan. She did as Zofia told her. And when the lesson was over and Mira took Rolf back from Zofia's arms, she left down the forest path exactly the same way she had always done.

Except this time, she didn't. This time, when Mira reached the point in the woods where she was out of sight of the house, she turned. She circled the loop through the woods that went nearly to the lake and then she followed the little stream that ran past Zofia's, walking back in the direction of the old lady's house, approaching this time from the north, instead of the south as she usually did. Because she was not going to the house, and she was not going to see Zofia. She was coming this time for Emir.

Emir was still at liberty in the sand arena. He had his ears pricked forward and was looking out through the trees, away from Mira, when she arrived. At the sound of Mira's voice, though, he swung himself round to face her and immediately trotted over to the rails.

Mira tied Rolf off to one of the railings. The little dog whined a little.

"Hey, Emir!" Mira called. The stallion stepped forward so that he was close enough to extend his swan-like neck and touch his nostril to the palm of

Mira's hand. "Wait here for me," Mira told the horse. She had tried once before to ride him, but that time she'd had nothing to hold on with and no way to steer. This time it would be different.

In the stables, she took the bridle off the rake. Then she walked back out into the arena, across the sand. Emir did not run from her but allowed Mira to slip the reins over his head and even lowered his poll to allow her to work the bit into his mouth and do up the straps, the throat lash and the noseband.

Gently Mira coaxed him until the horse was standing where she needed him to be, parallel to the rails of the arena. She climbed up to the middle rail and stood there, one hand on the rail to steady herself, the other bridging the reins across Emir's neck. From above, the horse's rump dapples looked like ripples in the water, spreading in concentric circles, the white centres inking charcoal at the edge.

Emir gave a restless snort and began to side-step, and Mira, seeing that her moment was slipping away and the horse was about to move out of range, took a deep breath and leapt.

She landed on his back lightly. She would realise later, of course, that the past week of learning to rise up and down with her hands on her head on a bale of hay had encouraged this lightness. And as soon as the stallion began to move, she felt her muscles respond in the way that Zofia had shown her, keeping her posture upright, holding her hands together, high and still. But she was still only walking, and now some squirrels had begun squabbling in the trees and Emir's attention was captivated by their infighting. He began to snort and back away, and then, without warning, he broke into a trot and Mira, who had thought herself up until that moment to be doing quite well, found herself bouncing everywhere and slipping in a rather slow and disturbing way down his left side. She grabbed a hank of mane to pull herself back up and right herself again, and in a split second Emir had shifted gear into a canter and, sensing that the girl had put him off balance, tried to fix it himself by changing legs, twisting his hindquarters into a disunited leap. The off-kilter stride threw Mira clean off his back in an arcing parabola and she landed face-down in the sand.

She couldn't breathe. She was gasping and heaving, struggling to get the air back into her lungs. The sand in her mouth made her gag, and still the air wouldn't come! She began to panic more, trying to suck the oxygen in through her mouth and nose and choking as her lungs refused to work. As she gasped for breath, she felt the tears well up in her eyes. She heard their voices and felt her throat closing over, desperate for air, as the girls held her: *Drown the Cockroach, drown the Cockroach . . .*

And she was fighting to get them off her. Except the hands on her now didn't belong to those girls from school, and the voice she could hear was Zofia, and she was saying, "It's OK, you're winded, that's all. You'll be all right, take deep breaths. Lean forward and put your head between your knees. Stay on the ground. There is no hurry to get up."

Mira did as she was told, partly to catch her breath, partly because if her head was between her legs, the old lady couldn't see her tears. And then, when her eyes were dry, she sat up again.

"Nothing broken, then?" Zofia asked.

Mira shook her head.

"You will have bruises, I expect," Zofia added, "but I think mostly what you've hurt is your pride."

Mira frowned. "What do you mean?"

"You thought you could ride him," Zofia said. "Even though I told you that you weren't ready."

The change in her tone, from comforting to cross, made Mira feel the tears might come again.

"I am ready," Mira shot back. "It's your horse that is the problem! Back home in Aleppo, I rode very well."

"I am sure you did," Zofia said. "On your slow plodders. This is what I have been telling you. Emir is not like them. He is a skyrocket. He is a supernova . . ."

"He is an unpredictable lunatic," Mira huffed, standing up and dusting the sand off her jeans. "No one could ride a horse like that."

As if realising she was talking about him, Emir pricked his ears and broke into a trot, snorting and throwing out his front legs as if to say, "That's me – untameable!"

Zofia chuckled softly as she watched his antics. And then she put two fingers in her mouth up to the knuckle and blew.

The shrill whistle that she made brought Emir to an immediate standstill. The grey stallion spun about on his hocks. Throwing sand up, he began to trot, this time over to Zofia.

"Yes, he is not easy," Zofia said. "I never said that he was. In fact, I told you he was difficult. His blood is hot, his paces are extravagant, his mind is quick, his talents are enormous. All of this makes him a most complex horse to ride. But then it is the complex ones who are the most rewarding."

Zofia stepped forward and took hold of Emir's reins and led the horse over to the rails. Still in her knitted slippers, her tracksuit trousers and a homespun jumper, she clambered up the fence, as well as a frail eighty-nine-year-old possibly could. And then, in a heartbeat, she was in mid-air and she had leapt from the fence on to Emir's back.

And suddenly the years disappeared from Zofia. On Emir's back she was no longer a hunched old woman. She was a prima ballerina, poised and graceful, her back ramrod straight, her hands held elegantly in front of her, as if she were carrying a silver tray set for tea. Those hands! They never moved. They stayed poised and still, no matter how much Emir skipped and danced beneath Zofia.

"We will warm up at the walk because he is tricky to engage at first," Zofia said as she walked past Mira. She clucked her tongue at the stallion, and gave him a tap with her heels, and Emir suddenly began to cross his legs sideways and step into a perfect leg yield.

"I begin his warm-up with lateral work to make him sharp to my aids . . ."

And now, as she said this, she moved the stallion into the most fluid and beautiful trot, except it went sideways – a half-pass, Zofia called it. Emir made it look easy and fluid as they danced one way and then the other. And then they were stretching out with long, flying strides across the length of the arena – an extended trot. Emir was snorting and arching his neck, and Zofia was so perfect and so still, and a moment later they were in the most spectacular bouncing canter that Mira had ever seen a rider perform, and then the horse was doing dressage moves – moves that Mira would only later know the names for: pirouettes, passages and piaffes. As the horse flung himself across the arena doing one-time changes in canter, so that he looked almost as if he was skipping from hoof to hoof, Zofia kept talking to Mira the whole time.

"This is not his forte," she was saying. "He is a show jumper, of course, but I like all my horses to be limber. Dressage is vital for all my show jumpers, from the babies to the Grand Prix superstars. My old horse, Embargo, the one I rode at my second Olympic Games, was so schooled on the flat he could just as easily have been ridden in the dressage."

"The Olympic Games?" Mira blurted out. "You rode at the Olympics?"

But Zofia was still focused on her riding, and she didn't appear to hear the question.

"Now Emir here, he is absolutely a jumper," she continued. "It's in his blood. All the same, I still often train him like this. It's good for his body and his brain."

As she was saying this, she had pulled Emir back to a trot and had slowly let the reins out long on the horse's neck so that he could cool down and stretch as she rode. Then she walked him a little until he stopped breathing hard, and then returned to Mira, who was standing, astonished, at the side of the arena.

"Seriously, you rode in the Olympic Games, for real?" Mira repeated her question.

Zofia nodded. "Three times I rode for the German team. And in so many FEI internationals. This was a long time ago, of course. And competitions are not everything, Mira. They are only a part of what makes you a rider. This is what I have been trying to tell you. I am not just training you to be a rider. I am training you to be a horsewoman."

"But why would you train me?" Mira found the words tumbling out before she could stop them. "I'm no good. I see how you ride now and I feel so stupid. You're right. I can't even stay on his back! I could never be any good!"

"You can be, and you will be," Zofia said softly. "If you put aside your ego and if you listen, then you will learn." She smiled at Mira. "Don't you see? You are me, little one. It is like looking at my reflection in a pond. A natural rider, and fearless too, but so wilful! Your instinct is already there – your ability is undeniable. But these natural talents need to be honed! I can do that. I can turn you into a rider, Mira, but only if you heed what I say! Learn control, discipline and true horsemanship. This is what Otto Müller taught me, and I will pass his lessons on now to you."

"Otto Müller?"

"Otto Müller was my trainer. He was the greatest show-jumping coach in the whole of Europe." Zofia paused. "If you think I am tough, you have no idea. Otto Müller was brutal. At first I hated him."

"Because of the Method?" Mira asked.

"No," Zofia said. "Because he was German. We met under difficult circumstances. But you will hear all about this when you come to me tomorrow morning and I tell you what happened after my return to Janów. Remember how when we last spoke, my brave dog Olaf was ready to kill a German on the doorstep of Janów? Well, now it is time for you to hear about the Colonel . . ."

## CHAPTER 8

### *Evil Unchecked*

We didn't meet on the best of terms, the Colonel and I, it is true. It was a rough beginning, certainly, when Olaf tried to attack him. But then you could hardly blame poor Olaf. He was not to know that the Colonel was not what he seemed. My dog had already faced the brutality of the Nazis when my parents were taken, and he'd come out of it barely alive. So when he saw the man in the German uniform emerge that day on the doorstep of Vaclav's house at Janów, well, he went berserk!

I hung on to his collar for dear life. Olaf snarled and snapped. His hackles all stood up on the back of his neck, his jaws open, the drool dripping, as he trained his black eyes on the enemy.

121

"I mean it. He's going to attack you," I warned the German officer again. "If you come any closer, I will let him go."

The German officer seemed surprisingly calm for a man confronted by a furious dog. "Don't be afraid," he said. "You have the wrong idea here. I'm not going to hurt you."

My eyes moved to the pistol in the holster at his hip. And then to the open doorway of the house behind him, where shadowy figures, men wearing the same uniform, were talking and laughing together. The house was overrun with German soldiers.

"Leave me alone or my dog will eat you!" I threatened again. But the officer was not even looking at me and Olaf anymore. He was staring hard at Prince.

"He's one of the horses that got loose on the road to the river, isn't he?" the officer said. "Thank you for bringing him home. I will take him now . . ."

Forgetting what I had told him, the officer stepped forward, and Olaf leapt at him. I could only barely restrain him and the man stopped in his tracks.

"Your dog doesn't seem to want me to get any closer," he observed drily. "We are at an impasse."

"Where is Vaclav?" I said. "I'll give the horse to him."

"Vaclav?" The German officer spoke as though he'd never heard of him.

"Vaclav is the head groom. He runs the stables."

"Of course, of course," the German said. "Well, Vaclav – he is no longer here. This estate is now under my command and my officers will take care of all the horses from now on . . ."

He went to take a step forward once more but Olaf lunged at him all over again, snarling and snapping, warning him back.

"Perhaps," the officer said, with his eyes on Olaf, "perhaps, for tonight, you should be the one to put the horse in his stall? There is a loosebox you may turn him out in – the fourth one from the end. Take him there and then, once you've made him comfortable, you can come inside. You look hungry and there is hot stew – I just ate some and it is very good. I'm sure we can find something for your dog to eat too, although if he does not like Germans, it might be best to leave him outside, as there are quite a few of us in there."

And with that, the German officer turned his back on me and walked inside the house. And there I was, standing in the driveway, all alone again with Prince and Olaf.

I could have run at that point, I suppose. But where

exactly was I running to? The Germans had taken over the Janów Estate, which meant, no doubt, they'd occupied the village too.

Besides, I had no energy or strength left to run. And Prince was exhausted and half starved. We couldn't have run any further.

All the same, it was good to see the colt perk up a little when the other horses in the stables called out to him. He raised his head and whinnied back, returning their calls, as if to say, "Yes, yes, I am home, I am home."

He seemed to know which loosebox was his. He headed straight for the open door on the right-hand side, fourth from the end, and walked inside. There was already water in the trough and hay in the rack, which made me sad, because it was obviously left over from when the estate had evacuated for the river and they had left everything exactly as it had been. So here we were, walking back in at precisely the moment when the grooms had realised the Germans were invading, and now, it was all waiting, as if the stall had been frozen in time for us. I thought about what the German officer had said about Vaclav, or rather what he didn't say. What had happened to all the men who used to work here? Where was everyone? And my parents – where were they? The Germans had taken them from our house, but I had no idea where they were now.

In the loosebox, I slipped Prince's halter off and let him go. He did not leave me straight away, but stayed close for a moment, nuzzling and nudging me with his muzzle, reluctant to separate. I couldn't decide whether it was because he felt scared to leave me, or because he felt protective. But the allure of the hay was too great for him to resist for long. Prince hadn't eaten for over two days now and he was starving. He strode across the stall and stuck his muzzle into the cradle, ripping a mouthful of hay loose and chewing it down ravenously. I was pleased to see him eating, but it only made me aware that I too was starving.

It had been more than two days since I'd had anything to eat or drink. And the hot stew the officer had mentioned did sound good. I'm not making excuses, but sometimes our choices aren't perfect, purely because there is no other option.

The stew was already on the table when I walked in through the door. The German officer beckoned for me to sit. I tried not to bolt it down without any manners at all, but I failed miserably. I was ravenous. The officer sat opposite me.

"I am the Colonel. I'm the head of these stables. And you are?"

"Zofia," I managed to say through a mouthful of stew, swallowing it down before I could add, "Zofia Bobinski. I live down the road."

I gulped another four or five mouthfuls in rapid succession and began to scrape the plate with my spoon. The Colonel gestured for me to hand my empty platter to him so that he could refill it.

I ate three whole heaped plates of beef stew and a big slice of strudel for dessert. Now and then, other men would walk through the dining room. They were German officers dressed in the same uniform as the Colonel. One of them, a man with slicked-back black hair, engaged in conversation with the Colonel about the health of the new horse. His name was Rudy, and the Colonel introduced him to me as their veterinarian.

When I had finished the strudel and another big glass of milk, the Colonel cleared my plates away and said, "We have no room here in the house, but I think perhaps you might like space of your own anyway? Above the looseboxes there's the hayloft. You could sleep there.

There's running water you can drink and wash with, and I can give you some sacks and a blanket and you could make yourself at home?"

I certainly liked the idea of being in a stable better than being in a house full of German officers!

Olaf was pleased to see me when I came back outside. The Germans had fed him too – meat bones left over from the stew. Olaf had gnawed them down to nothing but he still looked as if he could have eaten ten times more.

I took him out to the stables with me, but he didn't know how to climb the ladder up to the hayloft, so he slept on the concrete floor directly at the bottom that night. Prince was in his stall and the three of us, all exhausted by the past few days, and aware that each of the others was close by, slept deeply and soundly. It was a relief to all be together here, even though I was thinking all the time of my empty, abandoned house, and Mama and Papa and the staff of the stables, who seemed to have simply disappeared. But my exhaustion was so great that, even in my state of great fear, I slept. And when I woke, I looked out of the skylight of the hayloft. I could see down to the driveway and the house beyond and I noticed two things that I was certain hadn't been there when I arrived. The first was that the sentry box I'd ridden past to bring Prince home now had two armed guards stationed at it. And the second was that the flagpole that stood at the front of the stables no longer had the Polish flag flying. Instead, the flag that had been run up the pole was sharp black lines against white and red, the symbol of the Nazi swastika.

I went back into the house. The Colonel had assembled his men and was assigning tasks for the day, talking to them about feeding and exercise regimes for each of the horses, all of which was charted on a grid on the wall, with each horse individually named. I noted that Prince's name was up there with all the rest.

The Colonel released his men with a salute and then he turned to me. "Zofia," he said. "How was your night in the hayloft?"

The truth was it had been comfortable enough. But that's not what I said.

"I want to go home."

"I don't think that would be a wise idea," the Colonel said. There are SS soldiers everywhere in the village at the moment, and they may be at your house too."

"Who are the SS?" I asked.

128

"Hitler's special police force," the Colonel replied. "They are Nazis."

"Like you? Aren't you a Nazi?

It was a naïve question, I suppose, but I had just assumed from the German uniform he was wearing and the swastika that now flew on the flag outside that he must be too.

"I'm a German," the Colonel said. "But it is not quite the same thing. If you had asked me a few weeks ago – before this war began – I would have told you that I was a horse trainer and a show jumper. I was the commander of the German cavalry at Hanover, in charge of a hundred men and their horses. Then the SS came for me and said I had no choice in the matter. After all, I was a cavalry man, and Hitler was in need of soldiers in this war who understood horses. They said I would be posted immediately to run the estate at Janów Podlaski. Which is how you find me here."

"And Vaclav and the other men who were here before?" I asked. "What happened to them?"

"In truth, I do not know," the Colonel said. "The SS had cleared the stud farm before we arrived."

"What about my parents? I said. "Where are they?"

The Colonel hesitated. He looked around the room to

double-check that we were alone, and then he leant over the table and spoke quietly so that only I could hear him.

"Zofia," he said. "I have heard the whispers about what the SS soldiers are here to do. It is the same right now in every village in Poland. These SS soldiers, these men – they have their orders. Round up anyone who is educated – the academics, the politicians and the priests. It is felt that such people are a threat, for they'll be the first to stand up and lead an uprising if they are given the chance. And Hitler is too smart to allow that. So the SS have their orders. Round up the troublemakers in every village. Gather them together in front of everyone and make an example of them."

The Colonel looked at me. "Zofia, I cannot be certain, but I think your parents may have been amongst those who were taken by the SS."

I was stunned. I pushed myself up from the table. "But where will they be taken?" I asked.

The Colonel saw the look on my face. "Zofia, you cannot do anything now. I told you about the SS because I want you to realise how dangerous it is in Poland under their power. If you try to reach your parents, all that will happen is that you will be captured too. And Hitler's men, they have plans for children too. Even girls as young as you. They will drag you off to work in their factories. Try to help your parents, and you only succeed in putting yourself in grave danger . . ."He glanced at me again. "How old are you?"

"Nine."

"Back home in Hanover, I have a daughter. She is the same age, and has blonde hair and blue eyes just like you," the Colonel said. "I had to leave her at home with her brother and her mother, and I hope very much to see them when all of this is over. But know this: even if I were in the greatest danger, I still would not want my children to come to my aid. And I know your father would say the same. He would tell you to stay here and be safe. And you will be safe here, Zofia, I promise you. I have need of someone to cook for us and work in the kitchen and clean the stables. You could live in the hayloft. You would not be sent to the factories or the work camps and you would be able to stay with Prince and the horses."

I thought about the scene at my house when I'd found Olaf bleeding on the floor. They had taken my parents. I was certain of it.

"I have to go," I said. And before the Colonel could

say anything more, I was on my feet and out of the door, with Olaf bounding beside me.

As I walked the roads that led to the village square, I was passed several times by military jeeps filled with German soldiers, so I knew I must be going the right way. Other villagers like me were making their way there too. They were on foot and, like me, they all had haunted expressions on their faces.

The village square was already filled with people when I got there. The crowd was gathered round a platform that had been erected in front of the town hall. On to this platform there now stepped five officers of the SS, dressed in their black uniforms, with red swastika armbands. They stood and surveyed the crowd as more villagers gathered round. It was then that I noticed that there were German soldiers with guns standing all around the square, watching us.

"Good day to you, citizens of Janów Podlaski," one of the SS officers started. "You should know that Germany is a great admirer of your courage and bravery. You are proud people and we know it is not an easy thing for you to accept defeat and to hand over your village to us in this way. But as you know, the occupation of your beloved Poland is almost complete and the Third Reich is now in charge. So, we hope that you will welcome us without objection. That you will continue to be good citizens for us. Because if you are good, if you are well behaved, if you respect the power and the might of the Third Reich, then you will be treated justly. But if you fight back against us, if you try to defy us in any way, then things will not go so easily for you . ..."

As the SS officer said this last sentence there was a murmur from the crowd right beside the stage and I saw that the Germans were leading people up to the stage from the doors of the town hall. They brought them forward in a line. Ten people stepped up on to the stage and all of them wore black hoods over their heads. They were tied with ropes binding their hands behind their backs. The German officers manhandled them into posi-tion, right up to the very edge of the platform so that we could see them.

The hoods meant I couldn't see their faces, but I could see the rest of them – their clothes and their shoes. And two of them, two of the people bound and hooded in that row of prisoners, I recognised without question. For they were my mother and my father.

The head of the SS began to walk up and down the row. And when he reached my papa, I saw him lean forward with a smile and say something, a dark whisper in my father's ear. I can still see it in my mind, the way he cupped his hand to his face and told his black secret to my father. And then my father said something back to him and the SS officer's smug expression of delight disappeared and there was a grim, angry line where the smile had been a moment before.

All my life, when I think about that day, I always picture that moment and I always wonder why it was my father that the SS officer chose and what words were spoken between the two men, because after that he spun round with a click of heels and barked out to the crowd, "These people that you see here before you are traitors! They have been brought here today because they did not respect the absolute right of the Third Reich to take over Poland. They doubt the strength and the might of the Fatherland. They defy our right to rule, and today they will pay the price!"

And then he raised his arm straight out in front and he saluted and cried out, "Heil Hitler!"

All around him the Germans, all of them, they saluted too and they cried the same: "Heil Hitler!"

Then the SS officers on the platform shouldered their rifles and stepped forward. A murmur of terror rippled through the crowd around me. I could feel in the mood in the square that something very, very bad was about to happen. I saw the SS officer give the order to his men and the rifles were raised. And then I heard Olaf give a bark of fury and, before I could see what had upset him, I was snatched from behind by strong arms, grabbing me tight, lifting me up off the ground. A hand was slapped over my mouth so that I couldn't scream. Above the sound of rifles I heard the voice of the Colonel hissing in my ear: "Close your eyes. Close your eyes and trust me. There is nothing here that a child should ever see . . ."

***

Zofia stopped talking and wiped her eyes. They were damp with tears. "He was wrong, Mira! He was so very wrong. Because all of us, we need to see. If we do not look our oppressors directly in the eye, we can never truly defeat them. And that day, when the SS made my village watch in terror, that was the day that darkness took its grip on Janów Podlaski. We should have risen up and fought back right there and then. If we don't fight back as soon as we confront evil, it will only

135

grow and it will rise. And that was what happened that day. Evil found its power unchallenged and it took control. It would be a long time before that power would reach its end."

## CHAPTER 9

## *A Hundred Falls*

Mira walked through the school playground with her head down, staring doggedly at the ground. *Don't look up, don't make eye contact with anyone, keep moving as fast as you can, nearly there, almost out . . .*

\*\*\*

"You're so late that I thought you weren't coming," Frau Schmidt said when Mira arrived at the door. And she proceeded to fuss about for ages looking for Rolf's leash and collar, which she had misplaced, making Mira even later, so that by the time she reached the stables she was almost an hour behind.

"What time do you call this?" Zofia began to tell her

off, but then she saw the look on Mira's tear-stained face. "Is it something you want to talk about?" she asked. Mira shook her head. She didn't want to tell Zofia how the girls at school were bullying her.

"Very good," Zofia said. "Well, you are here now. Get him saddled up and let's begin."

"Me?" Mira said. "By myself?"

"Of course you," Zofia replied. "I'm making a horse-woman of you, after all. I'm not your groom. You need to be able to put tack on your own horse! Now go to it! Quickly!"

For the past week Mira had been practising tacking up on the hay bales. Putting the saddle on Emir was quite different. He didn't stand still like the hay did! He moved as if there were hot coals under his feet, swishing one way with his hindquarters as she tried to rest the saddle on his back, and then the other way as she attempted to pass the girth beneath his belly.

"Stay with him when he moves about like that."

It was Zofia, watching from the doorway.

"You see how he sidesteps away when you touch him?" she said. "He's testing you. If he tries to evade you, stay with him. Keep your hands on him. There! You see how he is standing still for you now, because you called his bluff? You can reward him for that by taking your hands away."

Mira did as she said and Emir stopped fretting and stood still.

"You established the rules and now he respects you," Zofia said. "A horse will always test boundaries with a new rider. Even before you're on his back."

She looked at Mira. "Well, come on, then! Finish tacking him up."

Zofia let Mira do the bridle and martingale, but the tendon boots she helped with, showing Mira how to tighten them so they were firm enough to stay in place, but not so tight that they restricted the circulation.

"Now your turn," Zofia said.

"For what?" Mira frowned.

"You can't ride Emir in jeans and trainers," Zofia said, handing Mira a canvas bag. "Here."

There was a pair of cream jodhpurs and knee-high brown leather boots inside.

"The breeches will be a little large, but that doesn't matter, as long as the boots are a good fit," Zofia said. "You need boots with a heel, or your foot will slip in the stirrup."

"These were yours?" Mira asked. And then she

handed the bag back. "I can't take them. I can't afford them."

Zofia frowned. "Borrow them, then," she said. "And do not make a fuss about it. Hurry up and get dressed."

Mira had never worn jodhpurs before. They were stretchy but firm as she pulled them on.

"The knee pads are a little low on you, but never mind," Zofia said.

The boots were the softest leather, almost like silk, and they fitted perfectly.

"They're Waldhausen," Zofia said. "The very best. Now –" she looked at Mira critically – "we'll have to tie back that ponytail of yours. I can't bear to look at that abomination bobbing around on the back of your head all afternoon. You can use my hairnet – then you'll look professional."

As Mira led Emir into the arena, she felt like her legs were jelly. The stallion no longer looked like the mystical creature she had first laid eyes on in the forest all those weeks ago. With his tack on, he had been transformed into a premier competition horse. Everything about him looked different when he was under the saddle. His profile, so delicate and Arabian, looked somehow more masculine with the defining black leather of the bridle, the noseband and browband adding weight to the slenderness of his face. The saddle, which Zofia proudly told Mira was a Pessoa, although Mira had no idea what that meant, was cut with a forward seat, so that the knee rolls sat against Emir's shoulders and made them look broader and more powerful. The martingale made his chest look broader. And the dark brown leather tendon boots on his legs contrasted with his pale grey coat to make him look as if he was ready for business.

"Mount up," Zofia instructed. Mira, standing on the sand arena, did it exactly as she had practised, time and again, on the hay bales, and found to her surprise that she could put her foot in the iron and swing her leg in a perfect and fluid way so that she landed lightly on Emir's back. The stallion stood perfectly still for her as she did so.

"Now, take him out to the edge of the school and allow him to stretch," Zofia said. "He's been cooped up in his loosebox, so he'll be stiff. Ten minutes of walking on a long rein is essential before we begin."

As Emir walked, Zofia began to do what she called "the tidy up". She began to ask Mira questions about her position. Was her shoulder in line with her knee?

No? Then fix it so that it was. Was there a straight line between her elbow and the bit? Yes? Very good. Could she imagine the string through the middle of her head, pulling her up like a puppet? Imagine it even more, sit up with her eyes looking ahead. Do not look down or your horse will go downhill. And we want our horses to be uphill at all times.

"And your hands, Mira," Zofia said at last. "Remember they are carrying the tray of china cups filled to the brim with tea. We do not want to spill a drop. Do it right now, or I shall be forced to bring out my real bone-china cups and make you carry them!"

All the time, Zofia kept talking too about Emir and what the horse was doing. She was explaining terms that Mira had never heard before. His hind hooves, apparently, needed to be tracking up. His front shoulder needed to swing. His quarters needed to be straight so that his hocks could drive under him. All of these things were like a foreign language to Mira, but Zofia made it so clear as she spoke that Mira could feel it! She could feel when she asked Emir to do something and the horse responded and felt a little different beneath her.

"You're going to ask him to trot now," Zofia said.

"Be prepared. His stride is so powerful it will throw you out of the saddle at first."

Mira asked for the trot and, as Zofia had told her, the stallion leapt forward at the lightest touch of her legs and Mira found herself thrown against the back of the saddle in the same way that an astronaut is pushed back by the G-force of a rocket accelerating.

Panicking, she dropped the contact on the reins and she must have tightened her legs, because Emir took all these signals as a sign that she wanted him to fling himself even faster and longer in his strides, and lengthen out into an extended trot. As he swung himself across the ground, Mira bounced and banged on his back and Emir flashed his feet out in front of him, devouring the sand arena beneath him with enormous strides.

"You can control this!" Zofia was calling out to her. "Stay with his movement. Half-halt him like I showed you! Collect him up, Mira! Now ask for canter. Uh-uh! Be very still in the saddle and sit down and hold your position and ask very, very quietly. Inside leg at the girth, outside leg back a little and squeeze! And there you go! How does that feel?

"Like flying!" Mira laughed.

Mira was not certain what happened next. One minute Emir was cantering and the next the stallion seemed to get a rush of blood. His strides began to get faster and then Mira realised that she had steered him towards one of the jumps that Zofia had set up in the arena. Zofia was calling out to pull Emir up, but the horse had the fence in his sights. Mira was trying to steer him when suddenly Emir refused in front of the jump, his front legs buried in the sand. Mira went flying straight over his head.

***

"Are you all right?"

Zofia's voice broke through the darkness. Mira opened her eyes.

"What happened?"

"You were unconscious," Zofia said. "Only for a short time, though." She knelt down beside Mira. "Can you wiggle your fingers and toes?"

"Yes."

"Are you in any pain?"

"No."

"Do you know what day it is?"

Mira thought hard. "Friday."

Zofia put her hand in front of Mira's face.

"How many fingers am I holding up?"

"Three."

Zofia rose to her feet. "You'll be fine," she said, "but I think that's enough for one day."

"I'm sorry," Mira said. "I didn't mean to fall. It was just . . ."

Zofia shook her head. "Mira, I am not ending the lesson to punish you. I would put you back on board now, except you were knocked out and with a concussion it's best that you don't ride for a day or two. But this is not . . . unexpected. Even with the hay bales, I knew it would be like this. When I told you that a horse like Emir is not for beginners, that is what I meant. Mira, you are going to fall off him. In fact, you will fall a lot." Zofia looked at Mira and, without any trace of humour in her voice, she said, "It takes a hundred falls to make a true rider. Trust me, if you can stay alive, then this will be good for you."

\*\*\*

It was dark when Mira walked Rolf home that night. She walked him to Frau Schmidt's, right past the shops and the school and past the park. And as she walked, she wasn't worried about school the next day – she wasn't worried about a thing – because today she had started the journey to become exactly what Zofia Bobinski had promised. She had fallen for the first time. Now there were only ninety-nine times left to go. She was going to be a true horsewoman.

## CHAPTER 10

### *Horses for the Führer*

The next day was a Saturday and when Mira arrived with her pen and book, Zofia had baked a fresh batch of angel wings and, for the first time ever, she offered one to Mira before she fed one to Rolf.

"Feeling better?" she asked.

"Much better," Mira said. "But I have a big bruise on my head. You see it?"

She pushed back her hair to reveal the purple welt.

"I told my mama it was from falling off the monkey bars."

"You always talk about your mother," Zofia said as she poured the tea. "But never your father. Did he not come to Germany with you?"

Mira found her throat closing tight so that she

147

couldn't swallow the biscuit. She had to take a moment to get her breath steady before she could reply.

"He was killed in the fighting. Before we could leave Aleppo."

Zofia nodded. "I am very sorry. It is a terrible thing to lose a parent. In Poland in 1939, the war made orphans of so many of us. Thousands upon thousands of children had no family. And for most, their fate was the camps and the factories. I was fortunate that day in the town square, when the Colonel came for me and took me back with him to Janów Podlaski. Without him, I would not have lived to tell this story . . .

\*\*\*

The Colonel put me to work, but it was not work at all mostly, because much of it, the parts with the horses, I loved. In the morning I would begin the day with kitchen duties. I'd make bread for the soldiers, then I'd move to the tasks assigned to me at the stables, carrying water and hay for the horses, and mucking out the boxes and turning the horses out, before going back to the house in the afternoon to peel potatoes and help the cook with dinner. Many of the soldiers under the Colonel's command had been members of his cavalry regiment back in Hanover, so they were true horsemen, and some of them were remarkable riders. They would drill their mounts in quadrille in the arena, riding four at a time in perfect harmony. I would watch them and the Colonel would give them instructions as they rode. I would listen to him refining and explaining the movements, and my basic grounding in dressage began there. In the afternoons, they would show jump over coloured poles, and again I would absorb the coaching the Colonel gave them from my position sitting and watching under the trees. the Colonel never minded me doing this as long as I'd finished mucking out the boxes beforehand. Sometimes he would even call me into the arena to stand alongside him as he coached, so that I could replace the poles in their cups if a horse knocked a rail.

The Colonel had four dedicated riders under his command who kept all of the horses exercised, and they each rode as many as five horses a day. Janów at this time had over a hundred horses. A few had been lost forever in the woods that day when the planes attacked. And of the ones who had made it home, some of these were too young to ride, including Prince.

"He should never have been ridden by you in the

forest that night. He is only rising two. That's too young to bear a rider," the Colonel told me. "As a rule, we start our horses just before they turn four. This is not only for the sake of their bones, but for their brain. Prince is not yet ready to learn the advanced moves that my men are in the process of training their mounts to perform."

He saw the look of disappointment on my face and then he continued, "But since you've backed him already and he coped well with a rider under the most testing circumstances, I feel he is wise beyond his years, and I see no harm in you riding him a little. You must stick to basic hacking though – nothing complicated that will bewilder him, but gentle rides in the countryside will be fine. After all, Zofia, you weigh no more than a feather. I hardly think the burden of a child your size taking him hacking down the lanes will hamper his development."

So I was allowed to ride Prince on condition that I used only a bridle, no saddle. "He's not ready for it yet," the Colonel said.

I didn't think anything of riding bareback. I'd ridden Prince with no saddle all the way home through a forest at night when we'd been getting away from the Red Army! And as long as I was allowed to ride, I would have agreed to anything.

It was slippery, though, to ride bareback, especially on a horse like Prince, who had a coat as smooth and fine as silk. And by now the colt was going through his 'terrible twos' and was quite inclined to spook at anything that moved. On our very first hack we went along the lanes that ran between the stables and the fields beyond. Prince spooked when he saw a pheasant, and I found myself flung to the ground so fast I didn't even know how I got there! I fell with such force that I was winded and gasping. Prince was so shocked at the sight of me lying there that he bolted across two fields before I could get him back. When the Colonel heard this, he told me that it was very bad manners for a horse to run when their rider falls.

"I do not mind the fact that you're falling off him," the Colonel said. "But when you do fall, please try to keep hold of the reins. You must train your horse to stand and wait for you to recover and remount." And then he looked at me and said, "It would be better, Zofia, if you did not fall off at all, but then we cannot expect miracles here."

At this stage I didn't know what I was missing, because I'd never experienced what a saddle even felt like. I didn't realise just how much they hold a rider in position.

A good saddle can do a huge amount to hide the faults and flaws in a rider's balance, and even when your seat is very weak, they keep you secure on a horse's back. I had no such luxury with Prince, and in that first year I fell so many times I lost count! That was how I learnt that falling is a skill as well, and a valuable one that all riders must learn. After a few times of hitting the dirt and having the guts knocked out of you, you begin to know how to tuck your body and tumble neatly as you strike the ground. You'll learn this, Mira.

You will discover how to fall, to keep your limbs free to break the blow, and how to ball yourself up to do a shoulder roll to absorb the shock of the ground. And you'll develop the mind of a rider with the emotional resilience to bounce back and get straight on board again.

So, anyway, yes, it was my year of falling, but I counted my blessings, because I was starting to understand now what it meant to be under German rule in Poland and the dangers that lay outside the front gates of Janów Podlaski.

Because Prince was too young to be schooled in the arena, the Colonel said I could hack him around the estate. Did he warn me not to go any further than the boundary gates? I think he may have said so, but one day, we were enjoying ourselves so much in the sunshine that when we reached the road we just kept going. And then I started thinking it would be good to see my village. The Colonel himself went into the village at least once a week for supplies but he never allowed me to go, and I suppose I was curious.

On the road I told myself that if I saw a German patrol, I would turn and go back, but all the way into town there were no soldiers or anything resembling a checkpoint. So I kept going.

When I saw the first signpost for the village, I thought it strange that they had replaced the Polish sign with a German one. Then, as I rode closer, I realised that all of the signs were in German. And in the café on the corner where my mother and father used to meet friends to talk about life, not only was the sign above the door in German, but there was another sign in angry red writing on the door, and this one read: NO POLES, NO JEWS, NO DOGS.

"Olaf," I said, looking down at my loyal hound, "that is you and me."

When I saw the Nazi officers walking across the square, smoking cigarettes and laughing together as if they owned the village, that was when I knew it was dangerous to be here. I turned and rode Prince at a brisk trot until we were able to slip along one of the back roads to enter the forest and ride through the trees to get back to Janów Podlaski. My heart was hammering the whole way in case there were Germans following me, and I never told the Colonel about what I'd done that day.

Sometimes, I thought the Colonel only kept me because I was useful. I was a good rider by now, and he would use me to train his green three-year-olds who had only just been broken under saddle. They were purebreds – young horses with bloodlines very much like Emir, powerful and expressive stallions who would have been a handful even for a grown military man, let alone a young girl. Yet the Colonel liked me to ride them, because my light weight on their backs and the softness of my touch on the reins was a gentle way of adapting them easily to ridden work.

The Colonel himself would often do this breaking-in work and even though he was a tall man with very broad shoulders, as a rider he was almost as light as me. I would watch him in the arena. He rode so gracefully. And once the horses were broken under saddle and he was schooling them to do dressage and to jump, then he began in earnest giving me lessons. I soaked up his methods like a sponge.

And if the Colonel was only keeping me because he needed me, then I cannot explain why he let me keep Olaf. After that day when my dog had threatened to attack him, the Colonel brought him round slowly, bribing him often under the dinner table with pieces of meat, hand-feeding from his plate. In the evenings when I went to bed in the hayloft, I had to call Olaf several times to get him to leave the Colonel's side, as he lay comfortably at his feet, beside the open fire.

There were winters by the fire and there were summers with the corn poppies in bloom when we would take the horses swimming in the river. After the year of falling, there was the year of schooling, when I taught Prince how to work under saddle, accept the bit and work through a contact. Swinging himself loosely, he would use his body well and listen to my aids. And then the next year, that was when he learnt at last to be a real dressage horse – to develop a powerful engine that drove him from behind. He learnt to be collected and magnificent. And then the year after that, he was strong enough in his back and legs at last so that I could teach him to show jump. We started on fences that were nothing more than cavaletti, progressing soon to poles that were at my waist, before tackling whole jumping courses that were higher than my head. Then we went on to jumps set to heights greater than the Colonel's own men were jumping. By the age of six, my horse was taking on Grand Prix fences. That is what the Colonel called them, although I had no idea what a Grand Prix fence was, as I had never ridden in a competition. How could I? There weren't any competitions to ride in during wartime! The German rule of Poland was brutal and so many – hundreds upon thousands – had died, and those who were left behind were starving. The Colonel had kept me cushioned from the grim truth that lay outside the gates of the estate. We always had enough food at Janów. When I think about the grain we gave the horses – it would have fed entire families of humans! The Nazis were always kind to animals; people were another story.

As I progressed through the stages of horsemanship, everything that the Colonel was teaching me shifted and changed, because, Mira, show jumping changes when the fences reach Grand Prix height. Over the little fences it's possible to jump in style by adhering to the basics and doing the simple crest release – just bending your body a little at the waist to tilt your balance forward and give the horse its head. But as the jumps become bigger, the whole game changes. You have to accommodate the height of the jumps by rising off the horse's back and standing with your backside in the air as if you are bobbing for apples! Even the old adage of keeping your heels low no longer applies. If you watch a lot of top international show jumpers, they almost seem to tip-toe in their stirrups and fling themselves at the horse's neck. All the same, the Colonel would scoff at such theatrics. He taught me how to jump in the style of the very best jumpers in the world – to keep position and tackle the huge heights and vast spreads whilst maintaining perfect balance. This is the way you can help the horse to travel through the air.

Over the years, I would jump many of the horses for the Colonel at Janów. I took nearly every horse in his stable round the Grand Prix course at some point. Some of them were amazing jumpers, it was true – and the bloodlines were extraordinary. But there was never another horse in that stable that I trusted or believed in as much as I did Prince. That horse! To be on his back was like riding with the gods. And together, him and I, we had something that was beyond the normal bond between a horse and rider. Our absolute trust in each other had been built under gunfire, in the pitch black of the woods, on the run for our lives from the Red Army. I would have given my life for him and he for me.

So although the war had taken so much away from me, it had given me this one perfect thing. It had given me my Prince.

And then, one night the Colonel told me with a grim face that he was expecting visitors.

It was not the first time the Colonel had hidden me. There had been other times over the years when the Nazi officers who occupied the town had come to see him and he'd made me stay out of sight.

But there was something sinister about the way the Colonel spoke of the 'visitors' this time. And who on earth would come all that way in the middle of the night in February when the snow was knee deep on the roads to Janów?

The hayloft, in a way, served as my 'summer house'. In the winter months I always slept downstairs with Prince. He would lie down on the floor of his stall and I would snuggle into the crook of his legs by his belly and tuck myself underneath his thick woollen stable rug. The warmth of his body would keep me from freezing, despite the bleak weather outside. Now it was February and I hadn't been up in the hayloft for months, so when I went up there that night there were cobwebs everywhere and the room was like an icebox. I dug a tunnel into the old stacks of hay and lined it with my blankets, intending to use the hay as extra insulation to stay warm. But it was still freezing up there and, by late evening, when the visitors still hadn't come, I was cold and I was curious. Who were these visitors anyway?

I tried to shove open the skylight so I could see outside, but the snow had fallen so heavily on the roof it was jammed shut by the weight of it. I couldn't see a thing from up there.

By midnight, when no one had come, I decided that the weather must have put them off and I went back down the ladder to be with Prince.

Not wanting the Colonel to know that I was disobeying him, I crept down the ladder in the darkness and made my way through the pitch black to Prince's loosebox. My horse had been lonely without me and we made a fuss of being reunited with each other – that was when the car headlights appeared. They shone in through the bars of the tiny window to Prince's stall, the beams bouncing off the walls, and, as they flickered, more lights appeared from the two cars that followed.

I could hear car doors slamming and then the Colonel's voice giving the Nazi greeting "Heil Hitler". With my heart racing, I crawled on my belly to the window and very carefully I lifted my head above the sill so that I could see. There were three black limousines and there was the Colonel, dressed in his full German uniform, saluting these strange men, and then I saw the swastikas on their car bonnets and on the red armbands of their black greatcoats. They were SS officers. My blood ran cold.

The Colonel and the SS officer spoke about the lateness of their arrival and then another man stepped round to the door of the car and opened it and a fat, bald man got out.

I could hear their conversation quite clearly and I remember how the Colonel's voice was taut and anxious in the presence of this man, how his Nazi salute went horribly wrong and so he clumsily offered his hand, which the fat, bald man refused. Dr Rau. That was what the Colonel called him. They began to speak about the horses and then suddenly the doctor turned towards the stables and they were on the move! The SS officers came too, their jackboots crunching through the knee-deep snow as they strode straight for me!

When they flicked on the hallway lights, going from stall to stall, I thought they would find me for sure. There was nowhere in Prince's stall where I could hide.

And then I looked at my horse dressed in his navy woollen stable rug. Oh, how my fingers trembled as I tried to unbuckle it from him! My hands were so frozen and I was shaking with fear.

At the very last minute I got the straps loose and I flung myself down in the furthest corner of the stall with the rug draped over me.

I could hear the voice of Dr Rau asking about Prince and the Colonel replied that he was undoubtedly the finest horse in the stables.

I shivered beneath Prince's rug as Dr Rau moved closer. I could see his polished black boots right beside me in the straw.

Dr Rau said that he was here for the horses. That he was the Master of Horses! Appointed by the Führer himself!

He kept saying that our horses belonged to the Führer now and that he would be taking the best ones from Janów, just as he had taken all the others. He had already handpicked Lipizzaners from Austria and Thoroughbreds from France. Now he was taking our Arabians to Dresden. There he was setting up a stud farm. The stolen horses were to be kept there and experimented on, selectively bred by Dr Rau. His aim was to breed them and create for the Führer the ultimate war horse.

The Colonel tried to object to him taking our horses but the Master wouldn't listen. He kept telling the Colonel that these horses were not his, they belonged to the Fatherland. That my Prince belonged to Hitler.

When I saw the Master had his hands on Prince it made my heart pound with such fury!

*Aryan*, I remember he called him that word. He said that Prince was so magnificent he would not be going with the others to Dresden, that Prince was going with him to Berlin. Hitler himself had a special plan for my horse.

That was the moment, Mira, that I knew Prince and I had no choice. We were in the greatest danger imaginable now. We had to run.

## CHAPTER 11

# *The Sommergarten*

A list of the things that Emir did not like: he didn't like to be kicked; he didn't like it if you checked him in the last two strides before a jump; he didn't like it if you came back down on to his back too soon after the jump. And he *really* didn't like it if you hung on to his head when he was trying to pop up into canter from a trot. And here is what Emir did when you did something he didn't like: he bucked. His worst ones were wild pig-roots that ended with a fiendish twist in mid-air that would have unseated a rodeo rider. Mira knew this now, because for the past eight weeks, she had found herself doing exactly the things that Emir did not like. And every time she touched a nerve with the grey stallion, his retribution was swift and

163

unyielding, and she would find herself eating arena sand as Emir flung her to the ground.

And yet. And yet . . . there were the moments in between falling – often they were very brief, it was true, but they existed. Moments of total glory, when she felt the acceleration and the power of the horse underneath her as Emir gathered himself and prepared to face down a fence, and she managed not to touch his mouth or to interfere but just sat there on his back in two-point position, waiting for the fence to come to them. Then she could sense that they were going to nail the perfect stride and she would stay poised and count him in to the fence the way Zofia had showed her – calling out his strides: one, two, three, four, five, six – and then they were in mid-air and it was beyond anything she had ever experienced in the world. It was glorious.

Despite the constant falls, they had progressed day by day – walking, trotting, cantering, working in two-point. Next it was over poles, and then over fences, small at first and then growing progressively bigger.

"It's not the height of the jumps that matter," Zofia would often remind her. "It is what you do *in between*

164

the fences. Any idiot can get their horse over one massive jump. But, Mira, what is the point of that? A Grand Prix course is not one single fence in isolation. The challenge is that there are many obstacles, and the great riders, the true geniuses, they come into that arena and see the whole course in their mind. You must ride in this way too, and know that every decision you make from the moment you throw your leg over the saddle is building to that clear round. The whole time you are focused on balancing the horse between fences and seeing a stride so that you can set them up to take off at exactly the right point. Even in mid-air over the fence, you should be already turning the horse and looking to the next jump."

"That would be easier," Mira replied, "if Emir would actually let me stay on his back. I've hardly ever finished a round without falling off."

"Ahhh," Zofia said cheerfully, "but look at how much better you are falling!"

There were two sides to Zofia, Mira decided. On the one hand, the old woman would drive and drive and drive her, never satisfied with Mira's performance. She would be constantly barking corrections at her, pushing her to tackle combinations of fences that seemed far beyond her scope as a young rider. But then Mira would find herself actually doing it! And on those rare occasions when Zofia did praise her, it was the best feeling in the world, because she knew how hard-won the compliment had been. So on the day that Mira rode Emir and took the stallion round a course of thirteen jumps, some of them set well over a metre in height, and she came rolling into every jump on a perfect stride and balanced him back neatly on his hocks to make the turns and had him straight into every combination and maintained the canter rhythm and never came back down too quick on to his back and had her eyes up and delivered a deft crest release jump after jump, all the way to the final combination, and went clear, she knew it was good. And as she brought the stallion back to a trot to cool him down, she heard Zofia say, "That was perfect, Mira, just perfect." And at that moment, despite the bruises and the hammering her spirit had taken over the weeks that had led to this point, she was happier on Emir's back right then than she had ever been in her entire life.

***

The day after her perfect round was the hottest one so far this summer. It was only 8 a.m., but already it was so warm that Mira's blouse clung to her as she walked to school. It was her favourite blouse, sheer and pink and short-sleeved. She had not really thought anything of wearing it, but when she walked into the classroom that day, Herr Weren gave her a kind of a double-take, and she realised that the blouse rather too obviously exposed the bruises she was covered in.

Herr Weren didn't comment on her purpled arms, but, during maths, when he came round to collect the exercise books, he paused to look at her in a rather odd fashion, and when the bell for morning tea rang and everyone was standing up to leave, Herr Weren called her name.

"Mira? Could you wait behind after class, please?"

There was an "ohhh" that swept over the class.

"Naughty Cockroach is in trouble," Leni sing-songed.

"What did you just say, Leni?" Herr Weren said.

Leni smirked. "Nothing, Herr Weren."

"Yes, well, we don't really need your input, Leni. You can go out and play."

Herr Weren waited until Leni and all the other kids had left the classroom, then he shut the door and it was just him and Mira in the room. He sat down on the corner of his desk and picked up a pencil, which he balanced between his forefingers as he spoke.

"Mira," he said, "I've been turning a blind eye to some of the behaviour that's been going on here since you arrived. But I don't know that I can do that anymore."

Mira felt sick. "Is this about my homework, Herr Weren? I will try harder, I promise."

Herr Weren shook his head vigorously and put the pencil down.

"No, no, no," he said. "I think you are getting the wrong end of the stick here, Mira. My concern isn't *your* behaviour. It's the behaviour of others towards you . . . Mira, I know you're being bullied."

"Herr W-Weren," Mira stammered, "no one is bullying me."

Herr Weren sighed. "Mira, come on. Every day for weeks, you've turned up at school covered in bruises, and then today I saw your arms and I think . . . Mira, I think you need to tell me who's doing this to you."

Mira's first thought was that this intervention would have been hilarious if it wasn't so tragically misguided.

And then, as Zofia so often told her, she saw what was really happening and it was as if the whole course was laid out in front of her – not just the single jump but all the fences. She was covered in bruises. Herr Weren did not realise they were from falling off Emir. All she had to do right now was to name Leni, to tell Herr Weren that the girl who had been bullying her mercilessly for the past year was actually the one who had done this to her, and she would have revenge. It was perfect. No one would doubt her story when she looked like this.

And yet . . . she just couldn't do it. She wasn't going to lie. "It's from horse riding," she said.

"Mira." Herr Weren stood up and walked over to Mira's desk, put his hands on it and leant over her. "It's OK. You can tell me the truth."

"I am, Herr Weren!" Mira said. "I've been learning to show jump, and the horse is highly strung and difficult, and I fall off all the time. I know how it looks – and I know why you might think someone else is responsible. But the bruises are my fault. I think they will happen less now. I've stopped falling."

Herr Weren looked hard at her. "You can see how unlikely this all sounds, can't you, Mira?"

"Yes, Herr Weren," she agreed. "If I was going to make up a lie, it would be better than this."

Herr Weren laughed. "That is probably true," he agreed. He stepped away from her desk. "OK, Mira. But, please – if you are having problems here at school, I want you to talk to me. And good luck with the show jumping. Please keep me updated of your progress."

"I will." Mira picked up her school bag.

"And stop falling off!" Herr Weren called after her as she left the room. "Put some chewing gum on your jodhpurs and stay in that saddle!"

As she walked down the corridor, Mira heard footsteps catching her up. She spun on her heels, expecting Leni to be looming behind her. But it wasn't Leni at all. A girl with dark hair. She had borrowed an eraser off her once in class and she knew her name – Frieda.

"I heard all of that," Frieda said. "Why didn't you do it? Mira, you had the chance. One word of accusation and you could have destroyed Leni. You should have taken her down."

Mira shook her head. "I'm not a liar."

Frieda shrugged. "If you had lied, I wouldn't have blamed you. Leni has been bullying you all year. She's got it coming."

Frieda took hold of Mira's arm and turned it a little so that she could see the biggest bruise. It was livid purple and ran almost from shoulder to elbow.

"You really should wear long sleeves, you know," Frieda said.

"It's too hot," Mira replied.

"Not to school," Frieda said. "When you jump. It protects your arms."

Mira looked at her.

"What?" Frieda laughed. "You think you are the only one who rides? I've got a horse of my own. His name is Indigo. We show jump – not like super-high, but I love it."

Frieda still had hold of Mira's arm and she let go of it now with a giggle. "My mum is taking me to watch the Longines Champions Tour this weekend at the Sommergarten," she said. "Come with me, if you like?"

Mira hesitated. She had a little money saved from walking Rolf now, but the Sommergarten sounded expensive. "How much will it cost?"

"Oh, we have a spare ticket! My sister can't come after all and none of my friends are horsey, and it would be so nice to watch with someone who gets it. Mum

171

tries, you know, but she's not a rider. So, yeah, Saturday afternoon. Meet at the train? All you need is money for hotdogs!"

***

Frieda's mum looked nothing like her. While Frieda was dark-haired and slight and tended to wear boyish clothes – stripy T-shirts and denim shorts mostly – her mother wore white jeans and gold jewellery and very big sunglasses, which she used as a headband to push back her sleek blonde hair. And where Frieda was shy and quiet, her mother was brisk and bold. She peppered Mira with questions.

"Roseneck must be very different to Syria?" she asked.

"It is," Mira said.

"Will you ever go home, do you think?"

"I . . ." Mira stumbled on the question. For so long, after they arrived in Berlin, she had asked her mother this and the answer had been, "Perhaps, when it is safe, when the politics change. Then we can go back." And then the years passed by. One, two, three, four, five, and now Mira didn't ask anymore.

"Maybe," she replied.

"Well, I hope the Roseneck residents have been very welcoming to your family. This is a very inclusive neighbourhood." Frieda's mother smiled.

Mira exchanged a glance with Frieda. Clearly her mother knew nothing about Leni and her gang.

"Yes, Frau Becker," she said.

They had good seats at the Grand Prix – in the stands, just three rows back, right behind the "kiss and cry", which was what the riders called the offstage area where the horses exited after their rounds were done and all the grooms and coaches and the owners were allowed to meet them and celebrate or commiserate.

When they arrived at the oval, though, there were no horses in the arena yet.

"The jumps look enormous," Mira breathed.

"Look!" Frieda pointed towards the Grecian columns that marked the far end of the Sommergarten oval. "Here come the riders."

"Where are their horses?" Mira asked.

Frieda giggled. "They walk the course on foot first. Have you never been to the show jumping before?"

"Oh, right," Mira said. She had watched Zofia walk

173

out and calculate the stridings on the jumps at home, but she didn't realise that the riders all did this before they brought their horses in. The riders strode across the sand together like old friends, which Mira guessed they probably were. Dressed in their jodhpurs, shiny boots and jackets, some wearing their helmets and some with bare heads, they laughed and joked and then turned solemn from time to time. Each of them stopped chatting to focus as they counted the strides between the triple combination, or marked out the shape they would take on the turn to the upright planks.

Now that the riders were standing beside the fences, the jumps looked even bigger.

"They're 1.65 metres," Frieda said. "That's Grand Prix height."

As the riders retreated, having finished the course walk, the announcer's voice came over the Tannoy. "And what a beautiful day for show jumping it is here at the Sommergarten. The best show jumpers on the European circuit will be in the ring today, starting with this man: Peter Holborg, and his twelve-year-old bay Holsteiner mare, Petit Bourgeois.

A man in a navy jacket rode into the ring on a stunning shiny bay horse with a perfectly pulled jet-black mane.

"Bags that one!" Frieda said.

"What do you mean?" Mira asked.

"We can choose a horse each that we wish was ours," Frieda said. "I choose this one."

Over the course of the next two hours, each horse that entered the arena was equally stunning. They took the jumps as if they had springs built into their hooves. There was such athleticism to their movement, in the way they got themselves out of tight spots and took the fences even when it was risky and there was a chance they might take a rail, or worse, bring the whole fence down on themselves. Every horse that walked into this arena was classy and expensive and elegant and fabulous and exciting. Frieda the horse-chooser changed her mind at least a dozen times.

"You can't own all of them!" Mira teased her.

"Why not?" Frieda laughed. "A Grand Prix show jumper like that? It must be worth – oh, maybe only four million? Five?"

Mira stopped laughing. "Really? These horses? They're really worth that much?"

"Oh, no!" Frieda said. "Some of them are worth

loads more! There was one horse, wasn't there, Mummy – the chestnut one that was ridden by that famous Brazilian rider – he was sold for fifty million to be used just to breed from. Not even to jump anymore!"

Frieda laughed at the look on Mira's face. "Anyway," she said. "I've chosen loads. And you haven't even picked one yet. If you could ride any horse round this course, which one would you choose?"

***

The Grand Prix was all Mira could talk about when she arrived at Zofia's the next morning. Her words tumbled out in a rush of confusion and excitement as she tried to describe the day: the tension in the grand-stands, the sound of the announcer's voice growing more and more excited as the six riders who had gone clear came back in for the jump-off.

"Did you really use to ride at competitions like that?" Mira asked.

"Of course." Zofia shrugged. "I rode on those very grounds at Sommergarten many, many times after the war."

Mira hesitated. She was afraid to ask, but Zofia anticipated the question anyway.

"Yes," she said.

"Yes, what?" Mira was puzzled.

"You want to ask me if you will be good enough one day. If you could ride there too. And the answer is yes."

"Really?" Mira's heart was racing. Then she said, "Frieda told me a Grand Prix show jumper is worth millions of Euros. But I looked at all of them and I would rather have ridden Emir than any horse that was in that arena."

Zofia was very quiet and thoughtful at this.

"In my time as a show jumper I rode so very many horses," she said. "I went to three Olympic Games. Our team took home the European Championship. For many years I had my pick of the best show jumpers in the whole of Germany, perhaps the world."

She smiled at Mira. "And now of all those horses, I think perhaps Emir, he would be the one I would choose too."

Mira smiled at this, until Zofia added, "Although there is one other. It would be hard to decide between them."

"Who is the other?" Mira asked.

"Surely you know the answer to this already, Mira?" Zofia replied. "Now, sit down with your notepad and stop gabbling! I need to finish my story . . ."

## CHAPTER 12

# *The Black Train*

In the darkness of the stables my heart was pounding so loudly that I imagined the Master and his SS officers would be able to hear it from the house!

"Did you hear what he said?" I whispered to my horse. "It's worse than we could have imagined, Prince. Hitler, the Führer himself, wants you now."

And that was when I knew what I must do.

"When the Master comes for you in the morning, you'll already be gone," I said. "You and I, we have no choice. We must run. We leave tonight."

As I saddled Prince in the darkness, I wondered where exactly we could run to. I decided we had to go west. Russian horse-eaters lay to the east. Beyond that, well, I really had no idea. Poland was in the Nazi grip and I'd heard the Colonel speak of the Red Army moving across the countryside too, so nowhere was safe, but all the same I knew that we needed to do whatever we could to put as much distance as possible between my horse and the Master and his plans.

I left Prince in his stall, tacked up and ready to go, and then slid open the big wooden doors that led to the driveway. From here I could see across to the lights blazing in the kitchen windows. I could hear the voices of the Germans drifting through the night air, the sound of dinner being served and glasses clinking.

I knew we had to escape, but my dog was inside that house and I wasn't leaving without him.

And then, just as I was contemplating how I could possibly get my dog out, the front door of the house opened! I ducked swiftly back behind the wooden doors of the stables just in time to be hidden from view as the Colonel emerged on the doorstep with the Master and two of the SS soldiers.

"Are you sure you want to leave tonight, Dr Rau?" the Colonel asked. "The snow is still falling and the roads are treacherous at night. If you wait until dawn . . ."

"Bah!" Dr Rau waved a dismissive hand at the falling snow. "This? It is nothing. I need to travel to Hostau immediately to oversee the stud farm. I will leave my men behind to arrange transport details for the horses. Thank you for dinner – it was . . . adequate."

The Colonel put out his hand to say goodbye and the Master glared at him and did not take it. Instead he gave the Nazi salute: "Heil Hitler."

At that moment Olaf appeared on the doorstep at the Colonel's side. He had his muzzle raised, sniffing, and he must have caught my scent on the air because he came running straight for me! Across the driveway and into the stables he bolted. The Colonel watched Olaf dash off through the snow towards the wooden doors. These had been shut before when the men had gone inside but now they were gaping wide. The Colonel must have known that it was me who had opened them and that I was the reason Olaf had left his side! But if that were true, he still didn't call the dog back to him or alert his men. He acted as though he hadn't noticed the open door, and turned the Master deliberately, taking him by the elbow to help him through the snow to his car so that he wasn't facing the stables, nor could he see the doorway. The Colonel shut the car door and stood and saluted the limousine as it pulled away, and then, with a knowing glance at the open stable door, he turned and went into the house, accompanied by the officers of the SS. I held my breath, wondering what would happen next, but a few moments later, the lights inside were turned off and now everything was darkness.

"Olaf!" I gave my dog a hug. "Good boy for coming to me! Clever dog."

And then I took Prince by the reins and led him out into the snow. It was time to go.

I had dressed as warmly as I could for the night-time ride. I wore three jackets, one on top of the other, that I had grabbed out of the tack room. And I had left Prince's stable rug on underneath his saddle to cover his flanks and ward off the snow. All the same, it was below freezing and even as we set out my fingers and nose were already going numb from the chill in the air.

At least the snow muffled the sound of my horse's hooves on the driveway. As Prince stepped out through the drifts, he sensed that there was something special about being taken out in the middle of the night, and he fretted and champed anxiously at his bit. Olaf, always obedient, stayed at my horse's heels, following loyally, his eyes bright.

It seemed to take us forever to make it down the

tree-lined driveway. The whole time I was expecting someone to notice that we were gone, waiting for the alarm to be raised and the lights to come on inside the house. But now we were almost there and once we were through the gates we could get off the roads as soon as possible and cut through the lanes that crisscrossed the estates around Janów Podlaski until . . .

"Hey you! Halt!"

I had been so busy looking back over my shoulder to see if anyone was following, I'd failed to notice the dark figure up ahead of us moving inside the sentry box.

"I said 'halt'! Put your hands in the air now!"

The SS officer stepped out from the box, holding the torch beam on my face, and I heard the unmistakable click of his rifle being cocked.

"Take this horse back to the house now. Turn round and make your way back immediately or I will shoot."

"How can I do that," I asked, "if I have my hands up?"

"What?"

"I need to hold the reins," I replied. "Otherwise I can't turn him round."

"Don't be clever," the officer snapped. "You can take the reins and turn him back to the house. But do not think to do anything to escape. I'll be following you."

The officer stepped closer and Olaf, who had been snarling this whole time at him with a low, rumbling growl, bristled and bared his teeth. I looked at the SS officer. He was young and he did not seem that confident with his gun. I was certain that if Olaf threatened him too much, he would shoot.

"Olaf, no!" I was firm with him. "Don't. Stay with me."

Olaf obeyed, and so we turned and proceeded back down the driveway, back through the snow the way we had just come, only this time there was a gun trained on my back.

The SS officer must have radioed back to the house, because up ahead of us the lights were being switched on and I could hear the voices of the men inside.

By the time we were back at the front door, the Colonel was standing there, flanked on one side by a couple of his own men, whom I knew well, and, on the other side of him, the five remaining officers of the SS, all of them with guns in hand.

"What is going on here?" the SS commander asked the gate guard.

"I caught this girl trying to take one of the horses," the guard said.

I knew what was coming now. I had been captured trying to steal the most valuable horse in the stables. There would be no escape for Prince tonight – nor for me.

And then the Colonel cleared his throat.

"There has been a misunderstanding, I think," he said.

"This girl is Zofia, and she is Prince's groom. The Master and I decided before he departed tonight that Zofia would be assigned to accompany the horse when he is transported to Berlin. The Master felt that a horse as valuable and as precious to the Führer as this one cannot be entrusted to men who do not know him or understand his temperament."

"Then why was she trying to leave with the horse in the middle of the night?" the guard asked.

"Ah, this is the misunderstanding, you see," the Colonel said coolly. "I asked Zofia to prepare Prince for the train journey and take him to the station. I told her the train would be leaving very early in the morning, but perhaps Zofia was rather premature in setting off for the station already. Her German is not always perfect, and she did not clearly grasp my instructions."

My heart was racing. He was covering for me! "Yes,

Colonel," I agreed. "I was taking Prince to meet his train. I'm sorry that I followed your orders incorrectly and caused all this trouble."

"Never mind, Zofia," the Colonel replied. "You had good intentions and no harm was done, I'm sure."

The SS commander narrowed his eyes at me, but he seemed to believe the Colonel's story. After all, why on earth would the head of the Janów Estate be lying to save the life of a fourteen-year-old Polish girl?

"Zofia, you may take the horse back to his stall," the SS commander said. "And you will wait there with him. In a few hours, I shall send my men to fetch you, and this time they will accompany you and the horse to be put on the train."

"Yes, sir," I replied.

And, under the watchful eyes of the officers of the SS, Prince, Olaf and I went back into the stables.

\*\*\*

As the hours ticked by towards dawn, I huddled in the stall with Olaf and Prince at my side, waiting for them to come for us. And then I heard footsteps outside and the bolt of the stable door being slid.

The door to Prince's loosebox swung open and there was the Colonel.

"Oh, thank heavens!" I breathed with relief. "I thought it was them!"

"They are not far behind me," the Colonel said. "The men are just finishing breakfast. We don't have much time, Zofia, before you go."

I didn't understand. "Before I go? But surely I'm not really going?"

"Yes," the Colonel said. "You are. I'm putting you on the train to Berlin with Prince."

"No! I thought that was just a story – about me being his groom," I said. "Something you made up to satisfy the SS commander."

"Zofia," the Colonel said. "Think about this. In just a few moments they are taking Prince, and if he gets on that train without you today, you will never see him again. This is the only way. I've tried to protect you, but the war is closing in here, for you and for Prince. For all of us. They say the Russians are taking over Poland. I can no longer keep you safe if you stay here. When the other horses go in the morning to Dresden, I'll accompany them. If you go with Prince, at least you will be together, and I will know that you have a chance."

In the darkness beside me, Prince pawed anxiously at the straw on the loosebox floor. I put out a hand to touch his muzzle and comfort him.

"You see?" The Colonel smiled. "He needs you, Zofia. Your bond with this horse is uncanny. It is beyond anything I have ever seen, and I think perhaps it comes from that night when you were lost in the forest and the Russian army were closing in. If Prince is to be taken to the Führer, then he will need you there to care for him. Tell me that you will do this?"

I nodded. "Of course I will."

By my feet at that moment, Olaf gave a whimper. I looked down at my dog and then I looked at the Colonel.

"Olaf should stay with you," I said, feeling a lump rising in my throat. "It wouldn't be safe for him to come with me."

Olaf cocked his head to one side. He had heard his name being spoken.

I worried that the Colonel would refuse. That he would say he had enough trouble managing men and horses without having some stray Polish dog being left in his keeping. But he looked kindly down at Olaf.

"I know what he means to you," the Colonel said. "You can trust I'll take good care of him."

"I know you will," I replied. "Just as you always took such care of me . . ."

And I felt my eyes blurring with tears as I said this. "That day, in the town square, when my parents were killed. You saved my life. And now you have saved it again tonight."

"It does appear," the Colonel said, "that we are making a habit of this."

He put his hand out. "Goodbye, Zofia Bobinski. Take care – of Prince, and of yourself too. I hope one day we will meet again when all of this is over."

I did not take the Colonel's hand. Instead, I flung myself at him and hugged him tight. And then, with tears making my face so hot and wet, and my chest so tight I could hardly breathe, I watched as the Colonel turned his back on me and walked away with my Olaf at his side, out of the stables and into the snowy night.

"Come on," I whispered to Prince. "You and I, we must prepare. We have a train to catch."

\*\*\*

The train station was eerily quiet that morning. I had expected it to be buzzing with people, but instead when

I led Prince in through the gates to the platform, there were no civilians – only SS officers flanking all of the entrances, standing guard, and several uniformed SS soldiers grouped together on the platform, looking tense.

I stood with Prince, surrounded by no less than eight black-coated officers. This was most certainly not the time for attempting an escape. And so I behaved like a dutiful groom, bandaging Prince's legs to protect them for the journey as we waited for the train to arrive.

We felt the train approaching before we saw it. There was a low rumble that reverberated through the platform and then the train came into view. It was jet black, and the engine sent out plumes of steam that carpeted the tracks and filled the air. It didn't look like an ordinary train at all. Behind the main engine, there was a carriage that looked like a tank, with anti-aircraft guns poking into the sky from its turrets.

All of the carriages after that were fitted with black-out-curtained windows to hide the passengers inside. I walked Prince along the platform. He was not yet accustomed to his leg bandages and was stepping very stiffly, with high steps. One of the SS officers helped me with his hay nets and water buckets, and another carried his saddle, bridle and rugs. At the end of the platform, two other officers were preparing a ramp that bridged across the tracks so that we could walk Prince into the carriage box. The carriage looked as if it had probably been a baggage car, but they had turned it into a makeshift stall, with straw bedding covering the floor. Prince was reluctant to cross the ramp at first, but I coaxed him to put one hoof forward and then another, and then he clattered across. He was a little distraught when the heavy metal door to the carriage was slid across to shut us in. But I was relieved, because at least it was just the two of us again, and we were no longer surrounded by SS officers with guns!

When the train began to move, I expected Prince to react, but he'd calmed down by then, and the sensation of the tracks clicking beneath the wheels was rhythmical, which he liked. I stayed at his side all the same, hand-feeding him his hay and speaking to him in a soft voice. Soon he settled down and began to tuck into his hay net.

The windows in the baggage car were small and barred. I had to move a water bucket over to climb up so I could see out – not that there was much to see. We had left the station now and the landscape that rushed past was nothing more than fields and hills, a little forest from time to time. I looked around the carriage. Apart from the tiny windows, which were too small even for me to crawl out, there were three doors: the big, heavy sliding door that Prince had been loaded through and, at either end of the narrow carriage, two small passenger doors for moving through the train. I jumped down off the water bucket and tried the doors. Both were locked. I climbed back up on the bucket again and watched the fields go by.

An hour went past, and then a second hour. The click-clack of the wheels upon the tracks became hypnotic, the scenery became monotonous. I lay down in the straw and soon I fell asleep.

It was only when I felt the wheels jerking and heard the hissing of the train pulling to a stop that I woke again. I did not know where I was. We had pulled into a large station. Surely it was too soon for us to have reached Berlin?

I climbed up and peered out of the window of the carriage. The sign on the platform was written in German, but the name of the city was Polish.

"We're in Warsaw," I whispered to Prince.

Prince raised his muzzle up to the open window and sniffed the air.

Then he turned to me and nudged me with his muzzle as if to say, "What's happening, then?"

"I don't know," I told him. "We've stopped, I guess."

I think they must have been loading someone or something else on to the train, because I could hear officers giving orders, but I couldn't see anything. And then there was the hiss of the engines and more shouting as the train moved off again.

We were about fifteen minutes out of Warsaw when the door at the front of the carriage opened and an SS officer entered.

"How is the horse doing?" he asked.

"He's travelling well," I said. "How much longer will the journey be?"

The officer did not answer my question. Instead, he put his hand on his holster and said, "You. Come with me."

We went back out of the door that the officer had entered through and crossed into the next carriage. On either side of the corridor were compartments, each one set up with beds along the wall. Four beds to a compartment. And on these beds were the neatly stacked possessions of the SS officers. These were clearly sleeping quarters.

"Hurry up." The SS officer prodded me to keep me moving ahead of him. I entered the next carriage and found that it was the same. More bed compartments lined both sides of the corridor. We crossed to the next carriage, and this one had toilets and showers.

"Do you need the toilet?" the SS officer asked me.

"No, thank you," I said. And then I added, "This is a very unusual train."

The SS officer seemed amused by this. "You do not know whose train we are on, then?"

I shook my head.

"This is the *Führersonderzug*," he said. "The Führer's own personal train."

My heart stopped beating when I heard this. "Hitler is on the train? He is here?"

"No, no." The officer laughed at this. "We are using the train on the orders of the Führer to transport certain . . . *important items* . . . to Berlin."

From the way he said "important items", I knew that one of these items must be Prince.

The officer opened the door to the next carriage. It was a grand dining room, with tables set with white tablecloths and crystal glasses and fine china.

"Would you like something to eat?" he asked me.

Mira, let me tell you, when you are on Hitler's own train – well, the food, it is very good. I had steak that day, which was something I had not eaten for a very long time. And potatoes. Mashed. And Sachertorte – which is a kind of Austrian chocolate cake – for dessert. And all the time, as I ate, the room was filled with SS officers, and they were all talking as if I was not even there! I guess they didn't care if a fourteen-year-old girl overheard them. Even so, their conversation wasn't very discreet, because they were on the Führer's very own train and yet they were talking about him, about Hitler himself, and about Germany, in a way I had never heard before.

"He has retreated to his bunker," one of the men was saying. "He lives almost entirely in seclusion there underground, giving orders. But he does not listen to the truth of how badly we are faring. The Russians are advancing. The Red Army are moving on Germany. Not even Berlin is safe."

*Not even Berlin.* I would remember these words a few hours later when the train pulled into its destination at Anhalter Bahnhof. For we were now in Berlin too. And the Russians, the horse-eaters, slowly but surely, were coming.

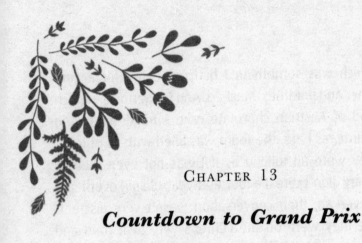

## CHAPTER 13

### *Countdown to Grand Prix*

Frau Schmidt had become accustomed to Rolf being picked up for his regular afternoon walks, but she was taken aback to find two girls waiting on the back doorstep.

"Mira!" she said. "You've brought a friend?"

*Friend.* The word sounded so strange and new to Mira, but wonderful at the same time.

"Yes, Frau Schmidt," Mira replied, "this is Frieda. She's helping me walk Rolf."

And so, with Rolf sweeping along merrily at Mira's ankles, the two girls strolled to the bus stop, then caught the bus three stops and took the sand tracks through the forest, turning away from the lake along the path that led to Zofia's house.

Ever since the Grand Prix, Mira had been dying for Frieda to meet Emir. Finally she had plucked up the courage to ask Zofia if she might bring a friend along with her to watch a lesson.

"I'm not running an after-school crèche," Zofia had grumbled. But then Mira had told her that Frieda was a rider too. "She's the one that I went to the Sommergarten with. I want her to see Emir."

And Zofia had objected a bit more, and so Mira had let the matter drop. She knew how private Zofia was. The old lady lived a virtually self-sufficient life here in the woods. She had her own chickens for eggs, and a vast vegetable garden. Zofia seldom, if ever, seemed to go into the city, or even leave the woods. And Mira still remembered how she had been that day when they first met, almost chasing her off the property. If it hadn't been for Rolf, of course, she would never have stood a chance.

And so she didn't press the matter. And then Zofia brought it up herself a few weeks later.

"What day are you bringing little Frieda to visit us?" she asked, as if that had always been the plan.

And Mira, heart racing, but not wishing to be too eager, said, "How about this Thursday?"

The walk to Zofia's was so much quicker with Frieda. They talked the whole way about show jumpers. Not the horses this time, though, but the riders.

"I have such a crush on Lukas Wexler," Frieda admitted. "Did you see him riding in that Grand Prix round on YouTube?"

"His horse is beautiful," Mira agreed.

"Never mind the horse! He's so cute!" Frieda said, slightly annoyed that Mira was missing the point.

"I suppose so," Mira said. "It's hard to tell when he's show jumping and he has a helmet on."

"Oh, I've seen him in real life. He came to my pony club once," Frieda clarified. "He's got really nice hair."

"What does really nice hair look like?" Mira said.

"Black and kind of wavy."

"Oh," Mira said. "Nice."

"Very nice," Frieda confirmed.

And, just like that, they were two regular friends talking about boys they had crushes on, and Mira found herself admitting that maybe some of the boys in their class weren't totally awful.

"Franz is OK. He lent me his ruler the other day in maths. And Noah. I talk to Noah sometimes."

"I went to kindergarten with Noah," Frieda said dismissively. "He blows snot bubbles."

"Ugh."

And so they returned to Lukas Wexler and his impossibly good hair. He also had very straight teeth – this was also according to Frieda, who had seen him at the pony club. And then, before they knew it, they were at Zofia's yard.

"Zofia, this is Frieda . . ." Mira did the introductions, but Zofia did not bother to even cast a glance at Frieda. She was busying herself with giving treats to Rolf and making a fuss of him. She grabbed the bridle off the hook. "I will fetch him for you this morning," she told Mira as she disappeared into the stall. And a minute later, she was back with the grey stallion in hand.

"This is Emir," Mira said proudly, watching Frieda's face – the way her friend's jaw literally hung open in disbelief at the spectacular beauty of the Arab, who danced on the end of the reins as Zofia lowered the stirrup irons ready for Mira to mount up.

"I wasn't expecting him to be like this," Frieda finally managed to blurt out.

"I know," Mira said. "That's why you had to see him."

"He is a handsome boy," Zofia said, giving the

stallion a pat on his neck. "But it is when he is under saddle that he is truly special. Come on, Mira, I will give you a leg up. We need to begin."

That day, Mira's lesson began with a warm-up using counter canter.

"It's a dressage move, but very useful to a show jumper," Zofia explained as Mira rode Emir around the arena in two-point to loosen him. "You are learning to balance the horse and make him strike off into canter on whichever leg you choose," Zofia said. "Now, there! You have Emir in counter canter. Now move his head away from the outside leg. Test his balance and suppleness by straightening him a little to the inside. Very good. Now on the other rein, and then we will work on landing on the correct canter leads over the fences."

Over the past months the jumps had got gradually higher and higher in Zofia's arena as Mira's confidence had grown. Today, the course was set at a solid height and there were many tricky turns.

"Softness, doing as little as possible to get a result – that is the way you must ride, especially with a horse like Emir," Zofia reminded Mira as she came in to the first fence.

"Don't waggle your head around like a bobble doll or yank at the reins to get him to land on the right leg. All you need to do is look the way you want to turn. In fact, all you need to do with him is *think* about the turn ahead and he will land on the right leg. Try it now. Very good. Now look to your next fence!"

That afternoon Mira rode into fence after fence and they never got it wrong. And Zofia kept putting the jumps up and up, and finally, in the last round, Mira found herself taking the upright planks with air to spare and suddenly realising that she had never jumped this high before.

"How big was that jump?"

"I'll check!" Frieda jumped down off the railing where she had been watching from for the past hour and ran across the sand to stand next to the painted planks. She used her own height to measure the jump. The top rail came up above the top of her head.

"I'm one metre sixty tall," Frieda said. "So it's more than one metre sixty."

Mira was stunned.

"It is Grand Prix height," Zofia admitted. "The rest of the course is not quite so big. Maybe one metre fifty? One metre fifty-five."

Frieda was still measuring the fence over her head, as if she couldn't quite believe it. "He just popped over it," she said. "He jumps all of them as if he has springs in his hooves. He is not a horse. He's a Tigger!"

Mira leant down in the saddle to wrap her arms round Emir's neck. "I know. He's such a star."

"You should ride him at Sommergarten," Frieda said. "There's a Junior Rider Grand Prix class coming up soon."

"Junior Rider?" Mira said.

"It means you have to be under twenty-one," Frieda said. "And the jumps are a maximum height of one metre forty. You could enter Emir. He would eat those fences for breakfast."

Zofia, who had been crouched down, fussing over Rolf, suddenly bobbed up and rejoined the conversation.

"When is this event, Frieda?" she asked.

"I'm not sure," Frieda said. "A few weeks away, I think. I have the Sommergarten calendar at home."

"Mira. Borrow the calendar from Frieda and bring it with you tomorrow morning when you come," Zofia instructed. "I will make enquiries in the meantime. I still have friends in the show-jumping world. I shall find out some details and pull together your entry and a training schedule."

Mira looked at Zofia.

"Are you serious?"

Zofia seemed surprised to be questioned on this.

"Do I make a lot of jokes, Mira?"

Frieda, not noticing how anxious Mira was looking, took Emir's reins to lead him back to the yard, and all the way she was talking with Zofia about the details of the Junior Grand Prix.

"I think the entries will close quite soon, so we would need to be quick," Frieda was saying. "And is Emir registered? If not, you might have to register him before you can enter, and Mira as well, and that will be an extra fee . . ."

"Hey! Wait!" Mira ran across the sand to catch up with them. "My mum will never pay the fees."

"Don't worry, Mira," Zofia said. "I am the horse's owner. It is traditional for the owner to pay such things – which means I get fifty per cent of your prize money."

Mira couldn't believe it – every objection she threw up was met with nothing but cheerful optimism from Zofia and Frieda.

"But I didn't even say I wanted to do this . . ."

"Of course you want to!" Frieda said. "Sommergarten? Mira! It will be amazing!"

Even Rolf was in on the excitement as they headed back to the yard. He kept leaping up on his tiny paws and yapping with delight as they went to put Emir in his stall. He was still racing around madly when they all went into the kitchen to make their plans over a freshly baked batch of angel wings. Rolf had four angel wings that day and his tummy was bulging on the way home through the Grunewald. Mira didn't eat a thing. She felt too sick with nerves. Zofia and Frieda had been adamant: this was happening. They were entering Mira and Emir for the Sommergarten Junior Grand Prix.

***

They had three weeks. This was the news that Zofia gave Mira when she arrived the following morning to work on the memoir.

"But that's not long enough," Mira squeaked.

And Zofia paused and put down her teacup.

"Mira," she said, "I know you want to do this. So why do you hesitate?"

"Because it's crazy," Mira said. "I've never competed

before. I can't go out there against all those professional riders on their million-dollar show jumpers."

"You think Emir isn't as good as their horses?" Zofia asked.

"No – I never meant . . . Of course he is," Mira said. "Emir is the best horse in the world."

"Yes," Zofia said. "He is remarkable. But he is not easy. Did I not tell you that when you first came to me wanting to ride him? I told you the risks, and yet you were willing to get on his back and to fall time and again until you were good enough for him."

"But that was different," Mira said. "No one was watching me fall."

"I was watching," Zofia said. "I saw how you committed yourself to the goal, and how you took the blows. Each day you would fall, only to get up and brush yourself off time and again. You never complained, and you never cried, even when the bruises made you wince in pain. Now, it is time to do it again. Get up one more time and face your fear. Put aside the demon of self-doubt, the destructive thoughts of failure. Think only of everything that *could* be. Because you could be one of the great competition riders of all time. But who will know if you never try?"

*One of the great competition riders of all time.*

That was what Zofia had said, and the old woman was not one to give compliments lightly – or at all, for that matter. So it had to be true. And Mira had no choice. She had to try.

From that moment, there was a change in Mira. It wasn't that she was no longer afraid. But she owned her fear. She turned it into a kind of excitement, and then she dominated it and controlled it. She made it part of what drove her to succeed.

As she trained and trained with Emir over the weeks that followed, she was learning a new discipline that hadn't occurred to her before. She was working on her own thoughts, blocking out negativity, looking at the course through Emir's ears and seeing her path shining ahead of her.

Not all the paths that lay ahead of her could be viewed through Emir's ears, though.

***

"Hey, Cockroach!"

Mira felt the spitball slap hard against the back of her neck. She didn't turn round. Leni was sitting behind her, two desks back to the right. It was her throwing the spitballs. Of course it was her.

"Cockroach!" Leni called again, her voice hissing insistently. "Cockroach, I'm talking to you. What's the matter? Don't you know your own name, Cockroach?"

A titter rose from the back of the class. Hannah and Gisela, brainless as always, laughing at their leader.

Another spitball hit her head just as Herr Weren walked back into the classroom.

"I have your essays here," Herr Weren said. "They have been marked. Can you please come and take them from me when I call you up?"

Mira shifted uncomfortably in her chair. She had written hers very late at night, after riding Emir, then taking Rolf home and helping her mother to make dinner for her younger brother and sister, so the writing had been a little hasty, but she had enjoyed doing it. The subject had been 'My Favourite Sport'.

"Some very good pieces were in amongst these papers I'm handing back," Herr Weren continued. "Particular standouts that I would like to mention are Franz and Nathaniel, who both wrote about BMX, and Noah, who wrote about football . . ." Herr Weren handed these essays back to the boys. "And Mira, who wrote about show jumping . . ."

Mira stood up to go and get her essay back. Herr Weren held it out to her and she saw the mark he'd given her. It was an A. She went to take the paper from Herr Weren, but he did not immediately let go.

"Mira," he said. "It sounds very exciting, this competition you'll be in. The Junior Grand Prix at Sommergarten?"

Mira didn't say anything. Her heart was slamming in her chest. She hadn't expected to be discussing her essay in front of the class.

"When exactly is this competition?" Herr Weren asked.

"It's this weekend, Herr Weren – Sunday afternoon at the Sommergarten."

The voice that had replied wasn't Mira's. It was Frieda's.

"This Sunday?" Herr Weren said. "Well, good luck, Mira. I hope you'll do well and we will have a few minutes where you can tell the class all about it on Monday."

***

"Why did you have to do that?" Mira was close to tears as she confronted Frieda outside the classroom afterwards.

"I'm sorry!" Frieda said. "I didn't think . . . I was just excited, you know? I mean, it's amazing that you are riding at Sommergarten . . ."

"Cockroach!" Leni moved dangerously close, her books clutched in her arms and her bag slung over one shoulder as she sauntered up to Mira. "Aren't you the teacher's pet?"

"Shut up, Leni!" Frieda shot back. "Just because you only got a C for your essay."

Mira saw Leni's face drop. And then Leni regained her composure and the evil smile returned. "See you at Sommergarten on Sunday!" she said. And then, as Hannah and Gisela joined her, they made mocking whinnying noises as they walked away.

"What did she mean – at Sommergarten?" Mira was panicked.

"Nothing," Frieda reassured her. "That's just Leni being funny, you know? She'll never show up."

"If she's there in the crowd watching me, I'll throw up," Mira said.

"She won't be," Frieda said.

Mira looked down at the essay on top of her stack of

books with the bright red letter "A" on it. She had written about show jumping in the same way that she felt about it. She had described the gruelling training, the gut-wrenching fear, the exhilaration, the million-dollar horses, and the glamour of competition. But mostly she had written about the bond between her and Emir.

*We do not speak the same language*, she had written. *He is from Poland and I am from Syria. But when we are together – when we are facing off against the fences, it feels like we are two halves bonded together as one in perfect unity. There is no one in the world that I trust more than him and no one in the world that I love more. He's my best friend. He's my everything. He is my Emir. And together, we are going to make history.*

She had been thinking a lot about history lately as she wrote Zofia's story. Now, each afternoon as she walked through the Grunewald to Zofia's house, she found herself anxious to arrive, to know the next chapter. The last time she had taken down Zofia's words, Hitler's private train, with Zofia and Prince on board, had just arrived at the Anhalter Bahnhof.

"When I stepped off that train," Zofia recalled, "the clock was ticking on the last days of the Nazis in Berlin. I didn't know the danger that Prince and I were in. But I was about to find out . . ."

## CHAPTER 14

## *The Bunker*

Anhalter Bahnhof station was so huge! Three enormous brick archways created portals for the trains to enter, with ceilings so high that the billows of steam seemed to create the illusion of clouds above us. I looked out of the window as the engines hissed and the brakes shrieked against the tracks and we pulled up to the platform. Uniformed Nazi soldiers were wheeling luggage trolleys forward to meet us, ready to unload the cargo. The SS officers on board the train were disembarking and giving orders, working their way down the train and opening doors until finally they reached us. The big doors were unbolted and the ramp was lowered and, through the steam and the bustle, I led Prince out on to the platform.

I stood there for a moment, not knowing what we

were supposed to do next, and then, through the crowds of German officers, I saw the Master of Horses striding towards me.

He looked as surprised to see me as I was to see him. I had thought he was in Hostau. And he, of course, until that moment, was unaware that I existed at all.

"You came out of the train carriage with Prince of Poland," the Master said. "Were you travelling in there? Who are you, child?"

"Zofia Bobinski," I replied. "I'm supposed to be here . . ." I cleared my throat and said with as much authority as I could muster, "The Colonel assigned me to look after Prince."

"A Pole? Why would he send you with him?"

From his tone of voice, my life hung by a thread.

"Yes, Dr Rau," I replied. "I've been Prince of Poland's groom for many years, and I know him better than anyone. The Colonel felt that the horse would be more relaxed and happier if I accompanied him. He has a very hot temperament that only I understand."

The Master's brow furrowed in consternation.

"Well, perhaps for the journey you were useful," he said, "but there is no need for your services any longer."

He reached out a hand to take Prince from me and

my horse jerked back away from him, ears pinned flat against his head.

"Hey, hey now . . ." The Master spoke confidently to Prince, but my horse was not convinced. He kept backing away until his hind legs were perilously close to the edge of the train platform.

"I don't think you should come any closer to him," I said.

Dr Rau glared at me. "You are attempting to advise Hitler's own Master of Horses how to handle a stallion?"

I said nothing more but tried to keep Prince from backing further as the Master came towards him. When the Master reached out a hand to grab the halter, Prince, with nowhere else to go, went up on his hind legs instead.

"Look out, Dr Rau!"

But it was too late. Prince was so swift with his hooves. My horse struck out and even though Dr Rau reeled back to get out of harm's way, the hoof still managed to catch him a glancing blow on his shoulder.

The Master fell back on the platform, and a group of SS officers ran to gather round him and help him back to his feet.

"Get your hands off me!" the Master growled. He was

still bent over, the pain making him cough a little as he tried to catch his breath, clutching his shoulder.

Prince, meanwhile, was dancing like a prize fighter who had just knocked out his opponent. He was weaving back and forth beside me at the end of the lead rope, and I kept nudging him forward, because he still very much looked as if he might plummet off the edge of the platform.

The Master stood up and caught sight of me gripping the rope and Prince skipping about furiously.

"Somebody take the horse from her before he is hurt!" he bellowed.

But these men on the platform were not horsemen. They were SS officers. And they didn't know the first thing about how to handle a stallion. They had already seen what had happened to the Master. If Hitler's horseman couldn't handle this beast, what chance did they have?"

"Take the horse off her!" the Master commanded again. Once more, his orders fell on deaf ears.

"Dr Rau." One of the SS officers, more senior than the rest, stepped over to help the Master to his feet. "The girl seems to manage him well. Why not let her take him to the Reich Chancellery?"

The Master turned on the SS officer. "You refuse to help me? The Führer will hear of this!"

The SS officer placed a hand rather deliberately on the Master's injured shoulder and gave it a good, hard squeeze. And I saw in that single, brutal gesture of domination that the power balance here was no longer what the Master expected it to be. The SS officer continued, "The Führer will hear nothing of this. Right now, he is in his bunker and surrounded only by the highest ranking of his officers. He will not speak to you, Dr Rau. I think we both know that he has much greater problems as the desperate situation of the Russian threat increases by the day."

The SS officer looked over at me and Prince. "We aren't horse babysitters. We cannot afford to waste any more time or manpower on your operations. So reconsider your position, yes? Because it seems to me, my good doctor, you have here a girl who can handle this horse, and you need a groom anyway. She will be useful to you in the days to come, I'm sure."

The tension between the two men was so palpable at that moment that it was as though they were locked in checkmate. If the Master backed down, he would lose face in front of all the men who had gathered on the platform to watch us.

There was deadly silence for a moment, and then I spoke.

"Excuse me, Dr Rau?" My voice was trembling.

The Master turned to look at me with incredulity, as if he couldn't believe I was addressing him at this moment!

"The Colonel sent me to you because I'm very experienced with horses. I was in charge of keeping his stables at Janów Podlaski. I know how to prepare stalls and feed and groom, and I'll work very hard."

Prince was not helping at this point, I must admit. He was still being dramatic and dancing at the end of the lead rope, looking as if he wanted to take on every man on the platform. I gave the shank of the rope a jiggle, as if to warn my horse to settle down, and this seemed to settle him. He stopped jig-jogging and stood beside me quietly at last.

As he did so, the Master stepped forward. He reached out once more, but this time not for Prince. His hand came down to rest on my shoulder and he spun me round so that we faced the SS officer together.

"I have no need of your inexperienced and inadequate men," the Master said to him. "This child handles a horse better than any of you."

The officer gave a wry smile. "Indeed. As you wish, Dr Rau. An excellent decision."

He turned to his men. "Give the girl some space to get the horse off the platform. Get back to moving cargo! Quickly now!"

And with that, the officers parted in front of us so that Prince and I had a clear path along the platform.

"There's a ramp you can lead him down at the far end." The Master fell into step alongside me. "From there we will walk him to the stables. Stretching his legs after such a journey will do him good."

He looked at Prince with admiration. "He's quite the athlete. It has been a long time since a horse was quick enough to get me off-guard . . ." And then he said in a darker tone, "It will not happen again."

The walk to our destination was along a broad, tree-lined road with tram tracks running through the middle of it. Prince's hooves chimed out on the street almost as loudly as the officious click of the boots of the troop of Nazi soldiers marching in unison in the opposite direction towards Anhalter Bahnhof. Dr Rau saluted them as they marched by and cried out, "Heil Hitler!" but I noticed that the men did not salute back or give a "Heil Hitler" in reply. They had such looks on their faces, as if the weight of the world rested on their shoulders. They were young, too – perhaps older than me, but not old enough to be soldiers, surely?

I thought about what the SS officer had said about the "desperate situation of the Russian threat". I wished more than anything at that moment that Prince and I were away from this place – that we could have been heading for Dresden with the Colonel and Olaf and the other horses, where we would have been safe.

Up ahead, there was a vehicle checkpoint to the left, and as we drew closer I could see the guard booths on either side were manned by armed Nazi officers. They immediately lifted the barrier to let us through, as if they were expecting us, and from here we walked on into an internal compound behind the walls. Now we were in a garden courtyard where, at the far end, there stood an elegant old building with a row of French doors and an archway. "Is that where Hitler lives?" I asked.

The Master shook his head and pointed to the ground. "The Führer is below us," he said.

"What do you mean?" I didn't understand.

"They built his bunker here," the Master said. "Seven metres beneath the surface of the earth. Those are the rooms where he resides."

This explained why the garden lawns outside the grand house weren't well tended and were made up of weeds and bare dirt. Why keep the gardens pretty when no one lived above the ground? Under our feet at this moment, Hitler was walking around with his generals! He was hidden away so deep in his chambers that the Allied bombs could not possibly reach him.

"This way." The Master led the way now towards the main doors at the end of the building. These swung open as if by magic, until I realised that there were guards on the other side who had been watching our approach. They were waiting for us.

And then we were inside and the doors were immediately closed behind us once more.

"Where are we?"

"The chambers of the Reich Chancellery," the Master replied.

"These are stables?" I said. They didn't seem like stables. The rooms were very grand and there was parquet on the floors.

"The Reich Chancellery was once used by Hitler as his private state rooms," the Master said. "But now, we are putting the building to other uses . . ."

He kept walking, leading the way along the main

corridor, setting a brisk pace. All the same, I had time to peer in through the doorways as we swept past. All those packing crates that the soldiers had been unloading from the train must have been coming here. There were rooms crammed from floor to ceiling with these wooden tea chests. In one of the rooms the containers were open and their contents were exposed, and in this brief glimpse as we raced by I saw golden vases poking out of the packing crates, and stone statues, and oil paintings, and I remembered what the Master had said about the Nazi's mission to steal away the very best paintings and famous artworks. And the horses too. "Living art," the Master had called them. But you cannot store a horse in a tea chest.

And none of these rooms resembled stables until, in the very rear chambers of the Reich Chancellery, the Master revealed to me a vision that I found hard to believe.

Inside one wing of this grand mansion, in a room with gigantic gold and crystal chandeliers and ornate high arched windows, a stable had been built. The room had been split up into a series of looseboxes, eight of them in total, four on each side down the length.

"This was once the Winter Ballroom," the Master said. "We converted it in this fashion because we knew that, while the compounds in Dresden and Hostau were relatively safe for the most part, we still needed to keep the very best horses as close as possible to the Führer to ensure their safety . . ."

Drowning out the Master's words at that moment came the sound of a horse's whinny. It was a clarion call, echoing through the stables. Prince, recognising the cry of another stallion, immediately raised his elegant head and responded.

And now there were other whinnies, more cries coming from the stalls, and the horses themselves began to appear, their faces up against the barred stallion cages that shielded their doors.

In the first box stood the horse who had made the call, and I was struck immediately by the sight of him, just as I had been that day on the road to the river when I had first laid eyes on Prince. Because this horse was magnificent. He looked nothing like my Prince – his beauty was quite different, as were his bloodlines, clearly he bore all the traits of a heavier-set breed. His neck was thick, with the crest of it considerably broader and more muscular than Prince's, making my horse look positively feminine in comparison. The proportions and angles of the face were unique too. The head was chunky, and in profile I could see that there was no dish to the face.

The horse had a Roman nose – that was what they called it – like an ancient sculpture, and slightly small eyes too, not limpid ponds like my Prince. And yet – it was hard to explain, but this horse had an almost ugly beauty about him. His mane was thick, and so long that it trailed right down over his shoulder. And he was not grey and dappled like Prince, but pure bone-china white, with pink skin showing through at his nostrils and muzzle.

"He's a Lipizzaner," I realised.

"You know your breeds." The Master was impressed. "His name is Neptune. He has classical bloodlines, the best in Austria. He's schooled in the airs above ground – the airborne leaps that only the greatest dressage stallions can master." He opened the door to the loosebox next to Neptune's. "This one can be Prince's stall," he said.

I led Prince inside and undid his halter, allowing him to wander at liberty, to take a drink from the trough and to pick at the hayrack. Behind me, I closed off the Dutch door – the bottom half was solid wood.

"You must always close the stallion cage on the top half as well," the Master instructed me, and closed this, locking off the steel partition on the top half so that Prince couldn't stretch his head and neck out of the stall. He was a prisoner behind bars.

"It's for their own safety," the Master insisted, when he saw my face. "So many stallions in close quarters like this will fight. If they can stretch their necks over the doors, then they can reach the stall next door to them and attack their neighbour."

I saw the sense in this.

"Come and meet the rest," the Master said. And he took me from box to box.

"These horses here are the Foundation Sires," he explained proudly. "Each of them has been chosen for their special traits, their physical appearance, and their athletic abilities. You have guessed the Lipizzaner; let us see how well you fare with the rest."

The horse in the next stall was more like my own Prince to look at, in that he was fine-featured, with a pretty face and deep, dark eyes with long lashes. He was a chestnut, though, with a coat as shiny as burnished copper, from which the light in the stable bounced, as if he were the sun itself.

"What breed do you think this is, then?" the Master asked.

I wasn't sure. The horse was tall, perhaps sixteen-two hands, otherwise I might have guessed Arabian. Also, his bone was more solid than Prince's, and his croup was less slopey, more substantial. Perhaps there was Thoroughbred blood in there too?

"Anglo-Arab?" I offered.

"A good guess," the Master said. "He is a Selle Français – the very best French sport horse from the small town of Saumur, where the Cadre Noir train."

The next stall contained a bay. He was not beautiful so much as ruggedly handsome – deep russet-red, with a jet-black mane and tail and a white blaze down his face.

"He is a Trakehner," the Master said. "A Warmblood from East Prussia that we managed to get out of Russia just in time. I like his refinement, this one. Still powerful, but so much more delicate than the heavy Coldbloods from the other regions. That is why I chose him."

The Master looked down the row. "There is another Lipizzaner in the last stall. You should meet him as well. Florian III is his name – quite different in many ways to Neptune, but with the same unmistakable traits of the breed. He will be a good additional Foundation Sire to keep the breeding programme fresh."

The Master walked down to Florian's loosebox and I looked inside at the pure white stallion eating his hay.

"He looks almost like a cross between Neptune and Prince," I said.

The Master seemed pleased with this assessment. "Exactly right," he said. "The bloodlines of the three of them, along with the Trakehner and the Selle Français, will be combined over the years to come. We'll find suitable broodmares so that we can experiment and cross-breed. In no time at all, we'll establish the new equines of the Third Reich, Germany's ultimate horse."

\*\*\*

I was given a room of my own just down the corridor from the horses, with a bed and a bathroom right next door. No other people lived in the building. I would find out later that this was because there was such fear of the Allied bombs that all of Hitler's staff lived underground. Horses, though, could not be taken into the bunker. So I stayed above ground with them. Which was fine by me – I had no wish to live like a mole. I slept in my room alongside Prince and the others – Florian and Neptune, and the Trakehner, whose name was Frederick, and Arnaud, the Selle Français.

225

Those weeks above the bunker were a time in my life when I should have been lonely, terrified and miserable, but to have such horses to care for made it all worthwhile. Every time I filled a water trough or stuffed a hay net and caught a glimpse of their beauty, I would find myself so transfixed that time would sweep away and suddenly I would realise I had literally done nothing but watch the horses for hours and hours.

The Master didn't like to take risks with the horses, but I convinced him that having them cooped up in their stalls all day long was bad for their well-being, so eventually he agreed that I could take them out one at a time and lead them around the gardens of the Reich Chancellery. Sometimes, I would see the soldiers doing much the same thing as we were, walking laps of the gardens to stretch their legs. They would smoke cigarettes, and as they huddled against the cold – for it was late February now and the weather was brutal – they shared gossip with each other and I listened in. Sometimes though, I admit, I ignored what I heard, because I did not wish it to be true. The soldiers were saying that Germany had all but lost the war. They were saying that Hitler himself was furious with his officers and that he had called his own generals "traitors to the

Fatherland". Down below in the bunker, things were rapidly falling apart. The next day, of course, you would hear a different story. Propaganda was spread so you never knew what was true.

***

For a few days now, the Master had been away. He had business in Hostau, he said before he left me, although he didn't elaborate.

And then he was back again. He came through the Reich Chancellery on the day he arrived back and gave the horses an inspection. And I'd assumed that was the end of that. But that same night, very late, when I was already in bed and the horses had been watered and fed hours ago, a Nazi officer came into my room and woke me.

"Get the horses ready for inspection," he told me.

"But he's already inspected them today!" I objected as I got out of bed, bleary-eyed.

"Move fast!" the Nazi officer barked. "They will be here in less than half an hour."

*They*. So it was not just the Master who was coming at this witching hour. There would be someone else with him.

I dressed hastily and headed along the hall to the stables. The horses were all in their rugs, but I took these off so they could be seen properly and brushed their coats to give them a bit of shine, running a comb through their manes. The last horse that I prepared was Prince and I was in his stall when they arrived.

The Master, I forgot to mention, had become a shadow of his former self by this time. He had lost weight, and his face, which had never been handsome, now looked like a bald skull. He was ashen pale and his usual brash arrogance – that sense that he relished being the most important man in the room – was noticeably absent that night.

The Nazi officers were going from stall to stall, poking the straw bedding with their bayonets, and it reminded me of that night in Janów, when I'd hidden in the straw beneath the rug in Prince's stall.

Now, as the Master and his companion walked into the room, the officers stopped and stood briskly to attention, and they vigorously gave their salute: "Heil Hitler!"

The man they saluted didn't return their salutes or speak in return. He ignored the soldiers and walked down the row of horses, peering in, stall by stall, working his way down one side and back again, until he reached the final stall, which contained myself and Prince.

I remember thinking, *Is this really him?* Because he looked so ordinary. He wasn't very tall – maybe a little taller than me. Skinny, with such bad posture, very hunched. And that weird little bristly moustache under his bulbous nose.

His eyes, though – those eyes, Mira, they were like staring into a black abyss of hate.

I had not led a sheltered life. I had met a great many men in that war whom I would have said were very bad people. But until that night in the Reich Chancellery, I had never locked eyes with pure evil itself. Not until I met Adolf Hitler.

## CHAPTER 15

### *Mira's Journey*

Mounted up on Emir in the competitor warm-up zone of the Sommergarten, Mira suddenly had the feeling she might throw up.

"I need to go to the bathroom," she said to Frieda. "Can you hold him for me?"

"Now?" Frieda said. "But there's only another four riders and then you're in the ring."

"I have to go!" Mira flung her leg over the saddle to dismount, and as she hit the ground she almost collapsed. Her legs were like jelly!

She ran across the sand until she reached the toilet block then pushed open the door of the last cubicle and locked herself inside. Leaning against the wall, she took deep, gasping breaths, unable to get the air into her lungs. There was no way. She couldn't do this. She wasn't going back out there. She sat down on the toilet lid with her head between her legs.

"Mira?"

Zofia's voice echoed through the toilets.

"Frieda said you ran off. Are you all right?"

*No!* Mira thought. *I'm really not.*

"Mira? Mira?"

"I'm in here."

"Do you want to come out and talk about it?"

"No."

"I could come in and see you," Zofia said, "but it would be quite cramped. Why don't you come out?"

A heartbeat, and then another, and then Zofia tried again.

"Mira, it will be very hard to ride your show-jumping round if you do not leave the bathroom."

"I'm not going to jump." Mira felt her voice choking up. "I'm sorry, Zofia. I just can't do it."

"It's OK, Mira." Zofia's voice was gentle, as if they had all the time in the world to be in this toilet block talking. As if the clock wasn't ticking down right now. But Mira knew there were at best three riders to go now before she was supposed to be in the ring.

"I won't make you go out there. This is up to you."

The door edged open a crack. Mira poked her head out.

"Hello – there you are!" Zofia smiled.

Mira opened the door the rest of the way and came out.

"So what has happened?" Zofia asked. "Why are we here in the toilets instead of in the warm-up arena with Emir? When I left you to go and fetch the number for your back, everything was OK."

Mira had been OK – even in the warm-up arena when she was being jostled and bullied for space by riders who were much more experienced than she; even when she had seen those riders on million-dollar horses being schooled over the practice jumps by their international coaches dressed in shiny boots and sparkling white jodhpurs and team jackets emblazoned with national flags. She had ignored all of that and focused on her horse. Emir felt wonderful. He was light in her hands and powerful in his hocks. He was snorting and champing at the bit as she eased him into his warm-up routine, trotting first and then cantering. She bounced him up into the strides, making him listen to her. The sound of the announcer on the Tannoy filled the air, calling the next rider in, and she knew she had just a handful of riders ahead of her. It was time to warm Emir up over his first jump, when . . .

"Cockroach! Hey, is that you, Cockroach?"

And she'd halted Emir and looked over at the rails by the footpath, where Leni was standing and staring at her with that twisted smirk she always had whenever she locked her sights on Mira.

"Cockroach!" Leni called out, as if this were the cleverest thing in the world. And then she hooted with laughter, and Hannah and Gisela turned up a moment later with soft drinks and hotdogs, and then they were all leaning on the rails and laughing at her.

"Just ignore her," Frieda had said. But Mira couldn't ignore her. She tried to, but she just couldn't, and she could see Leni's nasty little smile out of the corner of her eye as she brought Emir cantering into the practice jump, a simple oxer. She was so distracted that she felt herself losing her rhythm and over-riding at the last minute, clutching at the reins to correct the stride. Then Emir was sticking his nose in the air because he hated being interfered with in the final strides like that, and he was slamming on the brakes and planting his front legs deep in the sand, skidding back on his hocks and refusing at the fence. Mira felt herself being flung hard against his neck, getting winded a little, so that she very nearly came off. Her heart was hammering in her chest. She was in a panic now, and as she came back in to reface the jump, she kicked him on hard and flapped her hands, riding in a way she had never ridden before – ugly and noisy. She rode like she was scared, because the sick feeling in her stomach wouldn't go away. And Emir went over this time, but it was messy and he clipped the top rail with a hind leg, bringing it crashing down. There were more hoots of derision from Leni and laughter from Hannah and Gisela, and the other riders were staring at Mira now. She could feel their eyes boring into her back.

And that was when Mira decided she was going to throw up.

"*She's* here," Mira said.

"Who is here?" Zofia asked.

"The girl who bullies me at school. Her name's Leni. She's come to watch me. And now that she's here, it's like a hex, and Emir refused and I just know it's all going to go wrong and I'm going to crash or fall off or something, and Leni will be in the stands laughing at me and . . ."

And suddenly Mira was sobbing. Not just tears but sobs, great gut-wrenching, heaving sobs, and Zofia had her in her arms and she was holding her tight.

"I'm sorry," Mira sobbed.

"Not at all," Zofia said kindly. She lifted Mira's face to look at her and used the handkerchief in her sleeve to dry off her tears. "Do you know what?" Zofia said kindly. "I think we should have a chat about your life. We have talked a lot, you and me, over these past months together, haven't we? I've almost told you all of my story."

Mira sniffled and nodded.

"So now, while we are here and we have this chance, why don't you tell me yours?" Zofia said. "Tell me how you escaped from Syria."

Mira had not been expecting this. "You want to talk about it now?"

"Why not?" Zofia said. "After all, what is the rush if you're not going to ride? We have all the time in the world. So tell me the story. After your father was killed, and it was you and your brother and sister and your mother. How did you get out of Aleppo?"

"We didn't. Not at first," Mira said. "We stayed, because we had other family, cousins and friends. We weren't going to leave straight away. Mama thought we could carry on and live as we were, even without my father."

"So you stayed?"

"Yes, but very soon the fighting got worse and a bomb struck near our apartment, and my brother Rami, this time he got hurt. He had this wound on his stomach and they stitched it up, but after that Mama decided now we had to go. The bombs were too close and everyone was leaving. Many of our friends had gone already, crossing the desert to the border of Jordan, but we didn't go that way. Mama had managed to get us on a bus to Beirut. It was hot and crowded on the bus, and when we got to the city we slept in a dirty room. Then the next day we got the bus again, this time to Egypt. It was very, very crowded and hot and people were so crushed together inside we were like sardines in a can. Mama was worried, I think, that we would get turned away at the border, but the patrol let us in, and we made it to Cairo. I was so hot and dirty from being on the bus, and we hadn't washed in days.

"We were sent to a house that was full of families,

all sleeping on the floor, and everything stank, and we made food over a tiny Primus stove, and I remember not sleeping at night because everything around me was so strange and there were all these people in the same room as us – other women and children – and it smelt so bad and it was noisy. And then Mama went out one day and she left me in charge of Rami, my little brother, and Laila, my sister. And Mama was gone for hours. I thought, *What if she never comes back? What will I do? Should I go and look for her? But where would I even begin?* So I stayed with the others and by nightfall she came home, and she said she had met a man. His name was Aquib, and he was going to help us leave Egypt. Mama had given him all the money we had left – well, almost. Aquib had a boat, and he was going to take us from Alexandria on the coast of Egypt all the way to Italy."

"This Aquib," Zofia said, "he was a human trafficker?"

Mira nodded. "Yes, he made lots of money from smuggling people. I didn't know that at the time. He took us on the bus to Alexandria, and then he made Mama pay him even more money. She had no choice. And he tried to separate us. He said Rami had to go on a different boat because he was a boy, but Mama refused. Aquib threatened Mama. He was holding Rami's bag and trying to make him leave us, but Mama said no. If she'd agreed, I don't think we would ever have seen Rami again.

"On the night that we left Alexandria, it happened very fast. We were taken down to the docks and we got crammed on the refugee boat. There were hardly any life jackets, but Mama got one for me. We were crammed like sardines all over again, but this time on a boat, which was worse. There was no water or food, and the smell of vomit and machine oil, and no one on the crew would tell us how much longer it would take to get there. It made me claustrophobic, but when we had our turns up on deck to stretch our legs, the glare of the sun up there made me feel woozy, and I would look out at the horizon and the sun on the water would blind me and I would squint trying to see, but there was nothing to see. Nothing at all. And I would think, perhaps this man, this Aquib, has taken all our money and sent us off to sea to die. And one night there was a storm that was so bad that I thought the boat would go under and never come up again, and we were all going to drown for sure. But then the

morning came and we were still afloat and the sun was
out again and beating down harder than ever. And
then two days after that storm, we arrived in Italy. And
from there we travelled overland to eventually cross the
border into Germany and made our way to Berlin.
And when we arrived with all the other refugees, we
were sleeping in a tent, and each day we'd all go down
to the refugee centre together and wait in the queue,
and finally we moved to the apartment in the
Sonnenallee. Mama found the job at the bakery. But
she wanted us to be living somewhere where the schools
were good, and we would be safe and become more
settled, and that was when she got the job in the bakery
at Roseneck . . ."

"And then in the forest you found me," Zofia said,
"and you found Emir. And from the very first day, you
flung yourself at him without any fear. As I recall, you
spent every day for almost two months falling off. Your
body was one big purple bruise."

Mira had stopped crying now and she gave a hiccup
laugh at this. "I was a big bruise," she agreed.

"And yet, you never stopped riding him, did you?"
Zofia said. "You never once complained to me. Every
day I watched you as you got up off the ground and

dusted yourself off and got back in the saddle, and you became a rider, Mira. You triumphed because you never gave up.

"And so," Zofia said, "you are telling me that you were brave enough to go through all this – to suffer and fight to stay alive and be free and have a life that matters and to be a true horsewoman. You, Mira, are brave enough to have done all of this – and you are scared of some bratty little girl who calls you names? Because if that is the case, I think you should probably stay right here in this toilet, because you are not the girl I thought you were."

Mira's eyes were shining. "I'm not scared of her," she said. "And I want to do this. I want to ride."

"Good girl," Zofia said. "Then let's get out there. Your horse is waiting for you."

***

As they crossed the grass towards the warm-up arena Mira could see the rider in the main arena finishing their round. She was next to go!

"I can't do it," she said to Zofia. "He'll need warming up. He's not ready to go in . . ."

And then she looked at the warm-up area, where Emir was already warming up, cantering round the perimeter with a rider on his back.

"Frieda!" Mira waved frantically to her friend, but there was no need. Frieda had been looking out for her – she'd already turned Emir gracefully across the arena and was cantering him over to Mira and Zofia.

"Oh, thank god you're back!" Frieda vaulted off. "They're about to call your name. I've been keeping him ready for you, but I didn't know what I was going to do if they called you into the ring! Quick! Let me give you a leg up!"

"Thank you!" Mira said as Frieda vaulted her into the saddle.

"No problem," Frieda said. "Although he's quite a handful, isn't he? I mean, I knew he was a complicated horse, but I could barely control him in the canter, and he's so sensitive! I put my legs on and found myself at the other end of the arena! I don't know how you manage to ride him and make it look so easy!"

"You did great, thank you," Mira said distractedly. She had her attention focused now on the rider currently in the ring. They were just coming into their final fence.

"I need to get in there," she said nervously.

"It's OK," Zofia said. "Let them call you in. Don't be pressured in a mad rush. Take a moment. Deep breaths. Run through the course one more time in your head. Focus yourself, centre yourself, be calm."

Mira smiled back. And then she heard her name being called over the Tannoy and she stood up in her stirrups and rode Emir out into the arena in front of the crowd, with her heart beating like mad, no longer with fear, but with excitement. She heard the bell and prepared to begin her round . . .

## CHAPTER 16

### *No Horse Left Behind*

The Master walked over to Prince's stall and cleared his throat with a self-important cough.

"*Mein Führer,*" he said, "the horses in this stable have been gathered upon your orders. They possess the finest bloodlines in all of Europe. With these stallions, we shall breed the ultimate horse, one that will bring greatness to Germany."

Hitler peered in through the iron bars of my Prince's stall.

"Bring this one out," he said.

The Master hesitated. I knew he was recalling how violent Prince had been with him that day on the train platform.

"*Mein Führer,*" he replied, "perhaps you'd prefer to

examine one of the others? Neptune is the very best Lipizzaner stallion in the whole of Europe. I think you will find . . ."

"Are you questioning me, Dr Rau?" Hitler's voice had been calm a moment ago but now it was tipped with anger. Suddenly the Nazi officers were shifting about uncomfortably, as if they knew there was worse to come.

"Of c-course not, *mein Führer!*" the Master stammered. "It's only that this horse has a hot temperament – he's Polish Arabian and not the easiest to handle."

"Then you must ask yourself, Dr Rau," Hitler replied, "why such a horse is in your breeding programme in the first place. Perhaps, like the rest of Poland, he needs to submit to the will of the Fatherland or be done away with!"

Hitler turned to the two Nazi officers standing beside him.

"Go in there and bring him out!"

The SS officers looked terrified. *"Mein Führer?"*

"Do I need to give the order twice?" Hitler spat out the words.

The soldiers looked anxious as they slid open the bolts and entered the loosebox. Prince had backed himself to the rear of the stall by now, but the minute they entered, he came rushing forward on the attack, squealing and rising up on his hind legs, striking out at them with his front hooves.

"Argh! The beast is vicious!" One of the Nazi officers shouted at Prince. He fell to the ground and cowered in the straw, while the other made a feeble attempt to grab Prince's halter. Then Prince's hooves struck at him too and he retreated into a corner of the stall, edging his way to the door. Prince stood threateningly in front of him with his ears pinned back and tail thrashing in anger.

"Get those men out of there!" the Master shouted. "That horse will kill them."

That was when I pushed past the soldiers in the doorway of the loosebox and put myself between Prince and the Nazi officers, who were whimpering now, huddled in the straw.

"Prince." I held my hands up to him. "Shhh. It's OK. It's going to be OK."

I turned my head round to the soldier behind me. "Move now! Stand up slowly and leave the stables. I have you covered."

The officer on the straw scrambled out on his hands and knees, too afraid to even stand. The other one shimmied with his back to the wall until he was out of the door.

With the soldiers gone, the fury that had possessed my horse faded from his eyes and, although he was still snorting and fretting, he no longer had his ears flat or his tail swishing.

"Good boy." I put my arms round his neck and held him until he was calm once more.

"So it would appear that my officers are scared of a child's pony that can be handled by a little girl," Hitler snarled at his men in disgust.

"*Mein Führer* – that horse is crazy . . ."

"Excuses! Always excuses!" Hitler raved. "My entire army is full of weaklings who ignore my orders and run away at the slightest hint of danger. Is it any surprise that we can't halt the Russian advance on Berlin when you feeble fools can't even bring a horse out of a stable? Look how sweetly it behaves for a girl. A filthy Polish girl at that!"

"*Mein Führer*." The Master's voice was wheedling. "We have other Arabians you might prefer to this one. The horses that were sent to Dresden . . ."

"Those horses," Hitler sneered, "are already dead. The bombing of Dresden killed the Arabians that were sent there. And your priceless white dancing horses, the Lipizzaners in Hostau, have been stolen out from under our noses by the Allies."

"*Mein Führer*." The Master had obviously not known any of this, but he tried bury his shock and remain positive. "It is not over. We still have the best horses here. We can still breed the ultimate horse."

Hitler gave a nasty, hollow laugh at this. "Look around you, Dr Rau. The Third Reich is falling. We are losing the war because my own generals are traitors and their men are nothing but cowards. Berlin is being attacked. Soon, this entire compound will be overrun by the Red Army, and these horses too, like all the rest, will be dead. And for these ones, in the hands of the Russians their deaths will be slow and agonising."

Hitler walked down the row of the looseboxes and reached out a gloved hand to stroke Neptune's handsome cheek.

"No." He shook his head. "I am an animal lover, as you know. And I will not let the cowardice of my men allow these horses to be eaten by the Russian scum."

He looked down now at the German shepherd who stood obediently at his feet. The dog had been at his side since Hitler had arrived at the stables that evening.

He reached down and stroked the dog behind her ears.

"My Blondi. So good, so loyal. The Russians would brutalise you too if they had the chance, wouldn't they? But I will not give them that opportunity."

He looked back at the Nazi officers. "I will gather my dogs and I will have the vet feed them all cyanide. I will kill them all. Their deaths will be painless and swift. And these horses – they will die, too, before the Russians get their chance to eat them. Have your men dig a hole in the lawn of the Reich Chancellery outside the eastern wing. Make it deep enough for their bodies and then once it is done, take all the horses outside into the garden and shoot them."

"But, *mein Führer*!" Dr Rau was horrified. "*Mein Führer*, these are the best horses in all of Europe."

"Yes," Hitler replied. "And if they can't belong to Germany, then they belong in the ground." He turned back to his Nazi commander. "You have your orders. Carry them out."

"Heil Hitler!" the commander said. And the officers saluted and stood to attention as Hitler left the stables and disappeared back through the rabbit warren of staircases that led beneath the Reich Chancellery, down to the hidden bunkers below.

"You heard the Führer," the Nazi commander said. "In the morning at dawn you will get shovels and get to work – the hole will need to be big."

"This is madness!" Dr Rau tried to fight back. "We are all going to die. The Russians cannot be stopped. And now we are killing horses too?"

"We're following Hitler's orders," the Nazi commander said. "And if you don't want to end up in the hole too, Dr Rau, I suggest you leave us to do our work."

"These horses are priceless," Dr Rau argued back. "Would you destroy the *Mona Lisa*? I won't allow this."

The Nazi commander looked at the Master with dark eyes and then he turned to his men. "Escort Dr Rau from the stables and lock him in his room."

They took the Master forcibly by his arms, dragging him down the corridor as he kicked and shouted at them to let him go.

I expected that I would be next, but the Nazi commander was staring warily at Prince and suddenly I realised that they still needed me to handle my horse. Nobody else here had the nerve to get near enough to lead him outside when the time came to take him to the hole that was being dug for him. For this purpose alone, they were keeping me alive right now, but after-

249

wards, as soon as Prince was dealt with, it would be my turn. I'd be in the hole with him, and I knew it.

"You will care for these horses tonight," the Nazi commander told me. "In the morning, my men will dig as the Führer commands, and when we are ready, we'll come for you."

I watched as the soldiers marched out of the door. It had barely swung shut behind the last man before I was off and running, my breath coming fast as I sprinted down the stable corridor, heading for the tack room to grab Prince's saddle and bridle.

"They're going to kill us both!" I hissed at my horse as I re-entered his stall. "We have to go *right now*."

Prince danced beside me in the darkness as I threw the saddle on to his back and cinched the girth. I had the bridle on him too and was fumbling to do up the buckles with trembling hands when I heard the soft whinny of Neptune in the stall next door.

I stepped out into the corridor. Through the bars of his stall, I could see the beautiful white Lipizzaner tense and pacing across the straw of his loosebox. He kept shaking out his great mane in consternation, as if he knew that there was something going on – that everything had been decided and that his fate was sealed.

"Neptune?" I pressed my face up to the bars of his loosebox, my hands holding the rails as I called to him. "Neptune," I whispered. "I'm so sorry. I'm so very sorry . . ."

And then he came right up to me and I felt the velvet of his muzzle against my hand as he nuzzled my fingers and the hot, sweet clover scent of his breath on my cheek. And my eyes met his, dark like coal against his white face, and I knew at that moment that I couldn't do this.

"Wait here," I said, as if he had a choice in the matter. I ran again, all the way back to the tack room, and this time I grabbed the things that I needed out of the tea chest: a long lunge line, a lunge whip and four lead ropes. Then I ran back to Neptune's stall and fell against the bars of the stallion's cage as I worked the bolt. It was stiff, and it took all my effort to ease the shank of the bolt loose. Then I was in the stall and I had hold of Neptune's halter and I was leading him out into the corridor.

"I'm taking you with me," I told him as I threaded the lunge rein through his halter and clipped the lead rope to the shank.

Then I opened all the stable doors and, one by one, I

threaded the lunge and knotted it from horse to horse so that all of the stallions were tied together. For each one I had clipped a lead rope to their halter – Frederick, Florian, Neptune and Arnaud. "I'm taking you all with me."

It was crazy, I knew that. I had probably just sealed Prince's fate and mine too. I mean, if it had just been the two of us, it might have been an easy matter to slip away into the night. But to escape with five horses was an impossible mission. And yet I knew at that moment when Neptune's eyes met mine that I could not live with myself if I had left him there to die. It was all of us or none of us. No horse would be left behind.

***

A stallion's strongest instinct is to fight other stallions. In the herd, there can be only one stallion who dominates and owns all the mares. In the wild, stallions will fight to the death when confronted with one another. So to tie four of them together in a cobra formation, shoulder to shoulder, was madness.

They should have fought to the death, and I cannot

explain why the horses didn't try to kill each other that night. Perhaps somehow they knew that I was giving them their one and only chance to live, and that we were fighting against a force of darkness so great that, if we did not work together, we would all die.

*\*\**

I have never seen a more magnificent sight than those horses moving in unison, trotting out in formation like carriage horses, as we crossed the gardens towards the checkpoint at the entrance of the compound.

At the gates, two Nazi officers stood guard. I recognised them straight away as two of the men who had been in the stables earlier that evening with Hitler. They stepped out into the checkpoint to block my path. One of them lifted his rifle down from his shoulder, ready to aim it at me, but then the other guard put a hand up to stop him and shook his head. "Why keep them here to die?" he asked. The Nazi who had his rifle in his hand seemed to understand – after all, these horses were just a job to be done. Better to let us go and save the trouble of digging a hole.

The Nazi with the rifle eased his weapon back into

position on his shoulder and then moved into the sentry box before pressing the button to lift the arm on the checkpoint gate. I didn't wait for them to change their minds or for more soldiers to come – I was gone, out through the gates, with the horses in full trot, headed down that long tree-lined avenue that I had walked almost a month ago when Prince and I had first arrived here on the train at Anhalter Bahnhof.

Riding up front on Prince, I'd had a sense of freedom as we made it through the checkpoint gates, but now, approaching Anhalter Bahnhof and seeing the ruins before me, my elation gave way to despair. Anhalter Bahnhof was barely recognisable when I reached it. The gigantic brick arches had been destroyed almost completely by the Allied bombs. The surrounding streets were covered in rubble, and there were shallow craters where buildings had once stood. Burnt-out cars were abandoned on the roads.

And then I remembered Dresden. Hitler had said the city had been bombed and the horses were dead. He was such a liar, but why would he lie about this? And if the Janów Arabians had been killed, what of the Colonel, who'd been with them, and Olaf too? My sweet, courageous Olaf. So many nights I had wished I'd gone with them. Now I just hoped against hope that they had survived.

I trotted the horses on, keeping their pace through the streets beside the station to the river, and then headed west, crossing the bridge and finding myself on the broad paved avenues of a street called Potsdamer Strasse. Here, the apartment buildings that lined the wide avenue had their windows battened shut. There must have been people still in their homes, because I could see curtains being pulled aside to look at me as I rode by. I tried taking narrow side streets, but the damage left by the bombs made this impossible with four horses to lead. The wider streets suited us best, so I returned to the main road, to Hauptstrasse. Beneath me all this while, Prince was maintaining his stride, a steady, calm leader for the others. He stepped out with his ears pricked forward on the alert, and even when there was a plane overhead and we heard the bombs falling so near they were almost upon us, he never faltered.

We kept going along the Hauptstrasse, and up ahead I could see there was a pretty pink church next to a park. And right beside the church, spread across the road, was a roughly constructed roadblock of sorts. There were sandbags and these were braced with coils of barbed wire and the burnt-out shell of an old tram, which was being used as a barricade to block off one side of the street, so that I had no choice but to go between the barbed wire. I headed for the gap, and that was when I saw the barrel of the machinegun pointed straight at me.

"Halt!" a voice from behind the sandbags called out to me.

I pulled Prince and the horses to a stop, their flanks heaving.

"Please don't shoot!" I called out in German, hoping that whoever was behind the sandbags would recognise me as a friend rather than a foe. When that got no reply, I tried again, this time with one word. "Hello?"

From behind the sandbags I saw a helmet, and then the soldier stood up in clear view and finally I saw the gunman.

The uniform she wore was too big for her, and the helmet sat so low it almost hid her fringe, although I could see she had plaits tied with white ribbon sticking out at the back. Her hands were trembling, but it was hard to tell if this was from fear or because she was so small she could barely hold the weight of the weapon in her hands. This was not a Nazi soldier after all. It was not even a grown man. It was a girl, no older than me.

Blonde hair, blue eyes and fair skin. We could have been sisters, we were so alike. But there was one crucial difference between us, and this was not lost on either of us as she cocked the trigger: she was the one who held the gun.

"I'm supposed to shoot you," she said.

"Who says so?"

"My commanding officer," the girl replied. "He put me here with this gun and told me to shoot anyone who tried to get past."

"But I'm not coming into Berlin," I pointed out to her. "I'm going the other way. I'm leaving."

The girl looked confused by this. "I'm supposed to shoot you," she repeated. She looked as if she was going to cry.

"I know you are," I said. "But you don't have to. The war is over. You don't need to fight for them anymore."

"Hitler wants us to keep fighting," the girl replied.

I looked at her. She didn't look as if she knew how to shoot a gun. Somehow I felt that made her more dangerous. Her hands were shaking, and her finger was on the machinegun's trigger.

"I've seen Hitler," I said. "He was the one who told me what I'm telling you now – that the Germans have lost. The Russians are coming from the east and the Allies from the west. They'll be here soon and then they'll sack the city. You should go back to your family, and you should run."

"I don't believe you."

"I'm not lying," I said. "It's true. I promise you."

I could see she was looking at Prince, so I tried a different tack now. "I need somewhere to hide my horse," I told her. "Him and the others too. Is there anywhere near here? A farm? A stables, maybe?"

The girl hesitated.

"Please," I said. "I need to keep them safe."

She nodded, as if she understood at last the futility of our stand-off, and then she said, "The Grunewald. There are stables there."

She lowered her gun. "I will show you where to go."

***

All around me, Berlin was bombed out and burning, but the forest, the Grunewald, was peaceful and beautiful. The trees shimmered green against the blue sky and the birds sang here. I rode Prince along the sandy paths that led to the lake, the Grunewaldsee, and here all five horses took long, hearty drinks. I washed my face in the lake and cupped my hands and drank, keeping my eyes open the whole time, but there was no one watching us.

On the banks of the lake there was an elegant white building. It reminded me a little of the Janów Estate, with its long, low row of stables and the archway leading through to the castle. I rode Prince in, with the stallions harnessed to the lunge rope behind us, but it struck me straight away that the Russians might come here. It was too alluring – just the sort of place that marauding troops would enjoy occupying, putting their feet up and helping themselves to the wine and cigars stored in the cellars below.

Further into the woods, though, off the main tracks, I found what I was looking for – a tiny house. It was more of a small barn than a cottage, really, with a shingle roof. It wasn't anything fancy, and not the sort of place that would draw attention. But what made it perfect for me and the horses was that there was a stable block as well. Only three looseboxes, mind you. And I had five stallions, whose truce surely couldn't last for ever. They would definitely fight if they had to share a loosebox. So, despite my exhaustion, I spent the rest of that night in the forest with the axe I found in the woodshed, cutting down birch saplings and dragging their boughs back to the stables to build makeshift divisions, weaving the wood down the middle of the boxes so that two stallions could each have a separate half to themselves. There was some very old musty hay, which the horses were remarkably willing to eat, so the five of them slept that night with full bellies.

The next day I went fishing. There was a rod and reel in the house. I dug up worms for bait and I caught a good-sized trout. As it turned out, I would eat trout for breakfast, lunch and dinner in the days to follow, steamed and fried and smoked on the range in the house, which thankfully worked fine once I cleaned it up and gathered wood to burn in it. Another thing in the house that worked too, and this was far more important, was the radio. I managed to tune it in to Radio Berlin and would listen every day, waiting for news of the outside world. Often there was no news at all, just the solemn music of Wagner haunting me all day and all night. But then on May the first, the steady stream of Wagner was interrupted by shouting. The radio was yelling at me: "*Achtung! Achtung!*" Attention! Attention! And then more Wagner. I think the music was *Twilight of the Gods*. And then more shouting, and then the drum rolls began, and I knew that whatever was about to happen – the world was about to change.

There was a moment of absolute silence when I thought perhaps the radio had failed, but then the announcer's voice, cold and emotionless broke the news: *Adolf Hitler was dead.*

It would take another six days for Germany ultimately to admit defeat, but the death of the Führer was enough for me to know it was over, and that night, as the radio played Wagner and the drum rolls came again and again, I went out to the stables and threw my arms round my beloved Prince and wept for joy.

## CHAPTER 17

## *Grand Prix*

Inside the oval of the Sommergarten, Mira urged Emir into a canter and rose up into two-point, standing up in her stirrups in jump position. She shortened up her reins, checking him to steady his stride and he responded in typical Emir fashion by giving a high-spirited buck, flinging both his hind legs out in the air behind him. Mira barely moved in the saddle as he did this. She'd become so accustomed by now to riding the buck, it felt totally natural to her. And she didn't consider it a bad sign. Beneath her, Emir was so hot with excitement it was bound to fizz over a little. The key with a horse like him was to harness that energy in just the right way, so that when the fences came up before him, Emir was like a champagne cork – ready to explode for each and every jump.

Fourteen questions lay before them. That morning, after Mira had done the course walk, she had talked it through with Zofia. The old woman was so different here at Sommergarten. Mira had never seen her quite so serious or so glamorous.

They had dressed Emir for the occasion in a smart navy rug and white bandages, and Zofia matched her horse wearing white trousers and a navy gilet with a gold Longines Champions Series logo on the back. On her head there sat a navy baseball cap, also with "Longines" written on it, and a pair of black-and-gold sunglasses. It was only once they arrived at the venue and Mira saw the other coaches and riders in the warm-up area that she realised that Zofia's outfit was almost a uniform of sorts. Most of the other coaches here were dressed the same, with variations in team jackets for their countries or for their sponsors.

"How long have you had that jacket you're wearing?" Mira found herself asking.

"Oh, it's quite new," Zofia replied. "I wore it when my team took gold here in the Grand Prix in 1967. I think that was the last time I rode here."

"Has the place changed much since then?" Mira asked.

"Not really," Zofia said, smiling, gazing around at the Grecian pillars that led to the warm-up area. "It seems smaller maybe."

Zofia was no longer gruff and brisk with Mira. Here, amongst the other competitors, she became Mira's great ally – a tigress, fiercely protective of her rider.

"In the warm up, if a rider tries to barge you off your line, hold your track," Zofia had advised as they were walking back from picking up their rider number. "The riders here all know the rules. Pass left to left, and let the rider in the faster pace have the right of way. Don't let them push you around, because they will try. The warm-up arena is a place for playing mind games, and the other riders will do it sometimes just to psyche you out."

Zofia was even more tiger-like when it came to managing the officials. There was the moment a steward hastened over to tell Mira that Emir was not allowed to wear his ear nets – because they were illegal in competition. Zofia tore strips off him.

"FEI rules allow ear nets," she snapped. "Check your

own rule book before you come to harass my rider next time."

The steward had argued, but Zofia fought back harder, until eventually the steward had gone off to check his rule book before coming back and apologising. It turned out Zofia was right.

"I wasn't going to be bullied into taking them off," Zofia had grumbled. "Emir hates crowd noise, and the ear nets dull the sound and help him to focus."

She watched the steward, who had now turned his attention to another competitor and was harassing them about the length of their riding crop and whether it met regulations.

"There's always a little jumped-up Hitler like him at these events," Zofia had fumed as the official departed. "Trying to act important and tell you what to do."

Mira had noted the outrageous choice of words. A *Hitler*? Well, she supposed that if anyone had the right to make such comments about Adolf Hitler, it was Zofia. The old woman was, after all, in a unique position. As she had said to Mira, she had looked pure evil in the eyes and lived to tell the story.

When Zofia had given her account of that dark night

in the Reich Chancellery, Mira hadn't wanted to put down her pen.

"You'll be late for school," Zofia had insisted. "No more today."

Zofia had fed Rolf an angel wing and said goodbye to Mira at the door. "One more session, I think, and then we will reach the end."

But that final session hadn't happened, because the next day they'd been busy with show-jumping training and then this morning they'd had to be up at 5 a.m. to float Emir to the venue. Then there had been the plaiting-up and grooming. At 10 a.m. they had held the trot-up – which involved Mira dressing up in her best clothes and running down a concrete footpath with Emir beside her, so that the judges could confirm that her horse was sound and ready to jump today.

Then, after all the rush and the preparation, there was the interminable waiting around for her class. There were other jumping classes that morning, and Mira and Emir would not be competing until the late afternoon. Mira had sat in the horse float with her stomach tied in knots, thinking about what lay ahead. She'd been relieved when Frieda had finally turned up just before midday to be her groom. Frieda was wide-eyed and couldn't quite believe that she was backstage in the competitors' area.

"I've only ever been out the front in the grandstand before," she said. And she showed Mira the bright pink wristband she was wearing that indicated she was part of the crew. "Look! It's cool, huh? I'm going to wear it forever."

They had walked through the looseboxes together after that, looking at all of the horses, and then Zofia had come looking for them and taken them both out front to the public area, where she bought them all drinks and hotdogs and they'd gone to sit under the spreading oak trees on the green grass at the far side of the oval and watched the riders coming in to compete.

It had been the Team Grand Prix competition at that point, and Mira's favourite rider, she decided, was Anna-Maria Häkkinen, the bright-eyed young Finnish girl who was riding for a squad known as Team Unity. Häkkinen was a quiet, elegant rider, and she made it look smooth and effortless when her chestnut Warmblood put in the fastest clear round by almost two seconds. As she looked up at the clock and saw her score, she punched the air and the crowd erupted into cheers in the grandstands.

"She's amazing, isn't she?" Mira had watched the round with her heart pounding.

"The way she took that last fence with such a tight turn – I think that must have saved her a whole second."

Zofia nodded. "She has great technique. She is always looking for ways to tighten the course, for the best line to the fence."

Over at the kiss-and-cry, Häkkinen was met with great joy by a beautiful olive-skinned woman with lush waves of chestnut hair. The woman, dressed casually in a crisp white shirt and blue jeans, took the reins of the horse as Häkkinen vaulted off. She smiled with delight as they saw the time and first-place ranking on the board.

"Is she the horse's owner?" Mira wondered.

"She's the owner of the whole team," Zofia replied. "That's Princess Jana. She's the founder of Team Unity. Back in the day, the princess was an accomplished Olympic show jumper herself. Now she's more behind-the-scenes, which to me is a great pity. I did always love to watch her ride – she was quite something on a horse in her day."

There were superstars everywhere that Mira looked that day. Meredith Michaels-Beerbaum was here, riding on an elegant black mare called Apsara. British show jumpers Michael Whitaker and Ben Maher had both ridden clear rounds in individual classes earlier in the day. And the horses that these riders brought into the ring, one by one, were each more fabulous than the last.

"There are some exceptional bloodlines here," Zofia admitted, "but I wouldn't swap Emir for any of these horses."

She turned to Mira. "You have the best horse here today. Now it is time to prove it."

The course walk had taken place just after the lunch break. The jumps had been repositioned and set to a new height for the Junior Grand Prix riders – a maximum of one metre forty, with a maximum spread of two metres twenty. "There are fourteen fences out there," Zofia said as they looked over the rails into the Sommergarten oval. "Walk the line to each of them as if you are riding it, and walk the course exactly as I showed you to do."

Mira turned to Zofia. "You're not coming with me?"

"It is athletes only on the course walk," Zofia said. "That is FEI rules."

She smiled at Mira. "I've taught you how to walk a

course. You will be fine. Frieda and I will stay with Emir here and wait for you."

When Mira stepped foot on to the sand of the arena, she felt almost as sick as if she were actually riding the course. In fact, walking beside the jumps made her painfully aware of how enormous these fences were, and how demanding the twists and turns, the various combinations, were going to be. She tried to keep focused on her own game plan, on figuring out her route to each jump, but at the same time she kept her eyes and ears open, watching the experienced riders who were all walking their lines around her, intrigued to see how they would handle the approaches to each jump.

"Walking a course is an art in itself," Zofia had once told her. "Everyone does it differently. For me, the first time I walk a course, I look at each jump one at a time, and think about the stridings and break it down into components, think about how to ride each fence. The second time I walk it – that time I treat it as if I were actually on the horse and we are flowing our way from jump to jump in exactly the same way that we would do when we came in to ride."

On the second walk-through, Mira tried to visualise

riding the course on Emir. She felt like the most difficult fence might be the triple combination – it was right in front of the grandstand, so there would be distractions when they came in on the approach, and she would have to keep Emir's mind on the job. Fence one was a white-painted upright, two was a rainbow staircase, there was a broad yellow oxer that was fence number three, and fence four – the wall – looked tricky too. It had superimposed images of the Longines logo all over it, which could possibly spook Emir a little.

When Mira returned to Zofia, the old woman drilled her on what she was thinking and gave a few thoughts of her own. "The striding looks long in the double combination, and Emir strides short, so you will need to push him hard to make it," she said. "And those planks – the final fence – I feel that perhaps the horses will come in too deep for that one. It may cause problems."

Zofia was right – by the time the first four riders had been through, there was only one clear round. Two of them had knocked down a rail at the planks – the last jump. The third had a refusal at the wall.

"It's a tough course," Zofia had observed. "Luckily you are the last to go today. So by the time you come into the ring, you'll know what you're up against and you'll have to ask yourself the question, is it more important to take your time and go clear? Or do you need to push him to make the best time, knowing that it increases the risk of taking a rail?"

It was after this that Zofia realised that they had made the rookie mistake of leaving Mira's number back at the horse float.

"I'll go and fetch it," Frieda had offered.

"No. You stay here with Mira and I'll go and get it," Zofia had told Frieda. "I know my way around this place better than you do. You stay with Mira. Keep her calm. This is the stage in the warm-up when nerves can get the better of any rider."

Mira had been nervous as she warmed up. The jostle and shove of the warm-up had been scarier than she had expected. She had only ever ridden Emir at home on his own before, and she felt him spook a little as the horses got too close, and she was aware of just how athletic he was – if he wanted to, he could explode and put her on the floor here in front of everyone. And it was at about that point that she had heard Leni calling her. And then the toilets, and Zofia convincing her to come back out again. Now that she was back on board and entering the arena, not on foot this time but for real, with Emir bristling with energy and rolling into a powerful canter beneath her, the nerves didn't disappear exactly. They were transformed, from fear into something much more powerful. It wasn't anxiety that gripped her belly now. The knot was gone. In its place was adrenalin and the will to win, the urge to prove to all of them that her Emir, her bold, brilliant Arabian stallion, was better than any other horse here at the Sommergarten today. And in a mad rush she saw exactly what Zofia had always told her the best riders can see – not just one jump in isolation, but the whole course laid out ahead of her like a glistening prize. And she knew when the bell rang that she was ready. That *they* were ready to do this.

If she saw the course as a whole, though, Mira also saw each fence as a challenge in itself. She could not afford to drop a single rail in that ring today. There had been four clear rounds before her. And the times were all tight. Seventy-seven seconds had been the best time on the clock so far, so that was the time she needed to beat. Zofia had asked her the question: was it better to take her time over the course and play it safe, or to go flat out and take the risk of a rail falling as a result?

She knew now as she cantered and waited for her bell which one she needed to do. Speed today was going to win or lose the contest for her. Emir was naturally quick, but to make him fast enough to win, she would need to allow him to get a little hotter than she might usually like him to be, and there were risks associated with this hotness that even she could not calculate entirely. This was new to both of them – the excitement of competition. How would her horse react when she urged him to that first fence and the pressure was truly on?

At the bell Mira wrapped her legs round Emir and gave him a tap with the whip, just behind her leg, to let him know that it was game on. He responded like the hothead he was by flinging his hind legs up in mid-canter and giving a buck that was so vigorous that Mira found herself unseated a little, but she was soon back in sync and, as they passed through the start flags at a bold canter, with the first fence in their sights, she felt the adrenalin surge in her too. They took it cleanly, and now she was riding hard from the moment they landed, her eyes already on fence two, which required a hairpin turn, and then on from that, increasing the canter strides to get Emir really thinking about jumping big, because ahead of them was that wide yellow oxer. He took it perfectly, but his enthusiasm was getting the better of him now, and he was fighting Mira's hands every time she tried to check him and hold him back. If he hadn't been wearing the martingale to keep his head down, he would have smacked her in the face by now as he played against the reins, furious at being held back. Fences four, five and six raced past in a blur, and then, as Mira turned to come down to the triple combination, she felt Emir take the bit and surge. He was going too fast! He was flattening out. If she didn't check him now, he'd be able to get over the first fence perhaps, but he would flatten for sure on jump number two. She had to shorten up his stride and get his canter into a tight, energetic bounce again, but to do this, she needed to check him, and, more than anything, Emir hated to be checked in front of the jump.

What choice did she have? Mira sat up. And she took a pull and used her legs at the same time, as if to say to the stallion, *I know you are clever and bold, but, really, there is something very big coming, and, oh, please, Emir: Listen. To. Me. This once, let me tell you what to do.*

And Emir listened. He took the check and rocked back a little on his hocks, and suddenly the canter was balanced once more. He was charging in still, but it was controlled and beautiful, and he hit the first fence just as Mira would have hoped, on a perfect forward stride. Then she had her legs on him again, pushing hard to make the stride work to the second element, and then they were stretching out over the third. She didn't have the chance to even think for a second about how incredible it was that they had just pulled it off, because the Swedish oxer was ahead of them now. And then they had the tricky turn to the double, which she had talked about over and over with Zofia and decided she would not get risky here but go wide on the turn. Now that she was in the flow, it all changed, and she took the corner on the tight angle after all. Emir saw the fence in front of him and put in two neat, peppy strides and nailed it, and then they had the water jump in front of them. Mira no longer worried that he might find it spooky, but she rode it hard and direct nonetheless, giving him time to see the fence. His jump this time was so scopey – she felt him kick up his hind legs to give the rails air, and then she was already looking to her next fence, now turning in mid-air. There was one more big oxer, which they cleared easily, and then she was coming down to the final fence, the upright planks. And in the back of her mind she could hear the announcer over the Tannoy, saying her name:

"Young rider Mira Ahmad. She's inexperienced, but she's been training for this competition with the best in the business, famous German gold-medallist Zofia Bobinski. This is Zofia's horse that she's riding here today, the eleven-year-old Arabian stallion, Emir of Poland. As they come in to the final fence, they are clear so far and they are completely on the clock. Right now, this is Mira Ahmad's competition to lose . . ."

And then the jump was right there in front of her and Mira was thinking about the stride, looking for it, judging it, pushing for it. And Emir rose up underneath her and flew it, and they were clear and on the other side and pushing on for the finish flags. He gave such a buck as they went through them! As if he knew he had done it, as if he knew they always would do it just like this. And before she even looked at the clock, Mira reached down and gave him the hugest pat on his neck, and her smile was so wide that there was no doubt that Leni in the grandstand must have seen her grinning as she rode by. Then the clock was flashing and the scores were on the board, and she knew by the roar of the crowd before she even saw the time flash up herself:

76.4 seconds. She had beaten the best time that day by 0.6 of a second and she was clear. Mira and Emir had won!

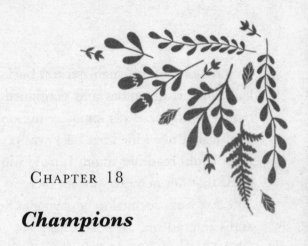

## CHAPTER 18

## *Champions*

It didn't really sink in when she was being congratulated by the other riders, or even when the TV crew were interviewing her. It was only once Mira was called back into the arena on Emir for the prize-giving – only when they placed the championship sash round his neck and handed her the trophy. It was only then that she believed it was real – as she rode the lap of honour, with the score flashing on the board next to her name.

She rode the honour lap standing high in her stirrups, with one hand raised in the air as she passed the grandstands. The faces flashed by mostly in a blur, and yet she clearly saw Leni, Hannah and Gisela as Emir cantered on. Her horse was right in front of them when he gave one of his high-spirited bucks. Mira laughed and ignored his antics and continued to wave to the crowd, who were clapping in unison to show their approval at her win. That buck was proof to Mira that Emir could read her mind. It truly was as if her horse knew that her nemesis was out there in the grandstand. *Take that!* Emir seemed to be saying as he shook his head and cantered on. *We're the champions, and she's just some dumb school kid, so sucks to Leni! She can't touch us anymore.*

The other riders who had placed second to sixth were called in to receive their prizes and lap the arena with her too, but they only went round once, following her. Then Mira rode round a second and final time on her own – a solo victory lap – before she followed the others out through the gates and into the kiss-and-cry. Frieda and Zofia were there waiting for her, and Frieda was fizzing with such excitement she was actually bouncing up and down on the spot.

"Oh my god!" Frieda shrieked. "You were unbelievable out there!"

"Emir is the one who was unbelievable," Mira said, giving him yet another pat on his glossy neck. "He did everything I asked of him. He's the best horse in the world."

Zofia, meanwhile, was crouched down by Emir's legs. She was checking his tendons. "His legs feel fine, but, just to be safe, we should put him in ice boots when we get back to the horse trailer," she said.

"I think I've got some StaySound with me to rub on his legs if you want?" Frieda offered.

Zofia and Frieda began to get engrossed discussing post-competition treatments for Emir, but Mira was no longer listening to them.

"Oh my god!" she murmured. "It's her. She's coming over this way!"

Through the crowds in the kiss-and-cry a smiling woman with lush waves of chestnut hair, wearing a white shirt and blue jeans, was striding purposefully towards them.

"Who is she?" Frieda wanted to know

"Princess Jana of Team Unity," Mira replied.

"Why is she waving at us, then?" Frieda asked.

The princess bounced across the sand, her smile growing wider still as she approached them. "Zofia? Zofia Bobinski! It is you, isn't it? I don't believe it – it's been so long!"

"Your Royal Highness." Zofia smiled as she greeted her. "It has been many years – decades, even. I think the last time I saw you was the World Equestrian Games in Stockholm?"

"Yes! When you were coaching Poland's team." Princess Jana smiled. "I remember how beautifully they all rode. You could always tell one of your pupils. They had star quality. It was as though you took riders and sprinkled fairy dust on them." Princess Jana looked up at Mira. "Speaking of starry – that was a very impressive display you put on out there today in the Junior Grand Prix."

"Thank you," Mira said. "I mean, thank you, Your Royal Highness."

Mira wondered if she should be curtseying. Or, in fact, how you would go about curtseying when you were on a horse!

"And this Emir –" the princess stroked the grey stallion on his velvet muzzle – "he's one of your homebred Arabians, Zofia?"

"He's from the Prince of Poland line," Zofia confirmed. "You were too young at the time, Your Royal Highness, to know his great-grandfather, my Polish stallion. He was the one that I rode at the Olympics, but he is just like him. The apple doesn't fall far from the tree."

The princess smiled at this and turned to Mira. "I heard the commentators sharing your story as you were riding your round. You know, I grew up in the Middle East in a small nation right beside Syria. And when I started Team Unity, one of my goals was to create opportunities for young riders just like you."

"I'm such a huge fan of Anna-Maria Häkkinen!" Mira blurted out.

"You are?" the princess said. "Yes, she's a lovely rider, and she's been a great addition to the team . . . Just as I hope you will be."

"Me?" Mira was stunned.

"Yes, Mira, you," Princess Jana said. "Well, you and Emir. I'm offering you a place in our squad. I want you to join Team Unity."

*\*\**

That night they returned to Zofia's, and Mira let Emir loose in the arena to stretch his legs while she went inside to prepare his stall. She mucked it out, laid fresh straw, then filled the hay feeder and the water trough. When she came back out, Zofia was sitting very still and quiet on a wooden bench by the railings, watching the stallion as he moved about the arena.

"He is quite something, isn't he?" Zofia sighed. "I often watch him and think how much he looks like his great-grandfather."

"I never knew," Mira said. "When you were telling me the story, I didn't realise that Emir was descended from him."

"Would you like to see a picture of Emir's great-grandfather, then?" Zofia asked. "I have angel wings, I think. It's a shame Rolf is not with us."

As they headed for the house, Mira realised that Zofia looked so much livelier than she had in a long time. It wasn't just the competition clothes – there was a spring in her step. And when they sat down in the living room, instead of tea, Zofia poured herself a "small nightcap of schnapps". For Mira she made hot chocolate to go with the angel wings.

From the dresser, Zofia took out a photo album. It had a plain white cover and in black felt-tip she had written on it in swirly text, *Prince of Poland*.

Inside were pictures of a grey stallion. In some of the images the horse was a pale dappled grey just like Emir was now. In other photos, taken when he had grown older, his coat had turned pure snow white. Often in the images he was standing alone, but in one picture there was a willowy young blonde girl with clear skin and piercing blue eyes beside the horse, staring at him lovingly and ignoring the camera. There were pictures of him being ridden in the show jumping too, soaring over massive fences, ridden by that same blonde girl.

"I look tiny on him, don't I?" Zofia chuckled. "And I think I've shrunk a little since then."

"Is that one taken at Sommergarten?" Mira asked, pointing to a picture where the horse was taking a water jump, knees tucked up high.

"No, that's in Paris. And that one is Hickstead. We rode internationally at all of the big competitions."

Zofia flicked the page over. "This is my favourite photo of him. He was only a yearling in this image – it was taken before I met him. I found it many years after the war was over when I had returned to visit Janów Podlaski."

"That's Prince?" Mira was amazed. "He's almost black – I would never have recognised him."

"Oh, it's him all right," Zofia said. "Look at the eyes! The dish of the forehead. He was always handsome, even then. He grew into his looks, though, filled out more. He was a skinny thing back then."

"You said you went back to Janów?" Mira said.

"I did," Zofia confirmed. She looked at the clock on the wall. "But it is very late. We should talk tomorrow."

"No, please," Mira said. "I'm not tired, and I want to know. After the war was over, what happened then? Please, can we finish your story?"

Zofia smiled. "I will put the kettle on for tea after all then. Grab your paper and pen and let me tell you my final chapter . . ."

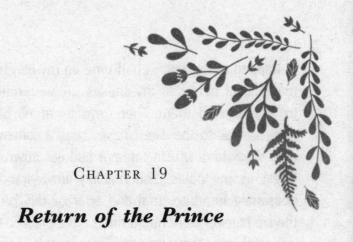

# CHAPTER 19

## *Return of the Prince*

At the end of the war, Berlin was in chaos.

I didn't dare to venture outside the Grunewald and, actually, even the forest itself wasn't safe. As I predicted, the Red Army had found the hunting lodge and soldiers had set up an outpost there. One time, on reconnaissance, they turned up at the cottage and ransacked the kitchen for food. My cupboards were empty – I was still living on trout and foraged mushrooms and berries – so they left again with nothing, but if it had occurred to them to look around the farm some more and go out to the stables, they would have found under their noses five of the best horses in the whole of Europe, and me cowering and weeping in terror in the corner of Prince's stall.

Trapped at the farm, I had time on my hands and five magnificent horses in my stables, so, with nothing else to do, I trained them. There was an arena back then, quite similar to the one I have today. I constructed my own show jumps, using trees I had cut down from the forest as my poles, and making jump stands out of household furniture. Trial and error quickly proved that the Lipizzaners were not jumpers – they lacked the physical attributes. Their cannon bones were too short, their necks swelled with massive crests, and their heavy haunches, so perfect for high-school dressage movement, were too solid for jumping. They simply weren't built for it, and so I worked instead on my dressage with them. The Colonel had shown me the basic movements when I was his student at Janów, and had given me a book detailing the advanced moves. I would never have mastered these on my own, but now I found myself progressing purely because the stallions were already experts, so they were the ones teaching me. One day, asking Neptune for a lengthened trot, I put my legs too far back, and instead he began to piaffe for me, leaping up and down in the air on the spot. It was magical. Another time, on Florian III, I was asking him to do a simple change in canter, and suddenly we were doing one-time changes and skipping across the arena. In this way I became a dressage rider – the techniques those horses taught me were more advanced than I deserved and gave me a lifelong love of riding flatwork, despite being a show jumper at heart.

Aside from Prince, the Selle Français, Arnaud, was my best jumper. He was scopey and fearless. Once, at the Sommergarten, I rode both of them in the Grand Prix round and ended up taking both first and second place! Prince had won, of course. I don't think Arnaud ever beat him, but he certainly came close.

As the war days receded, no one came to claim the cottage, and so I stayed. It became safe to venture into Berlin, and I would make regular trips into the city. I needed money to feed myself and the horses, and I found myself a job at a local stables not far from Anhalter Bahnhof, of all places, where the carriage horses were kept. It was like my old days at Janów Podlaski, mucking out stalls and mixing hard feeds, grooming and tacking up. The men who ran the coaches were horsemen too, and they talked to me. It was from them that I heard that Hitler had been telling the truth – the bombing of Dresden had killed many of the horses from Janów. But there were rumours that some had survived, and so had the horses at Hostau, taken by the Americans, who now had claimed them as "spoils of war".

There was a call for the horses, like the great artworks that the Nazis had stolen, to be returned. All across Europe, the stud farms were asking for their stallions to be given back. But the Americans did not return them to Janów. Perhaps there was concern that the horses would end up in Russian hands.

Meanwhile, I had the five horses in my stables in Grunewald. They weren't mine, I understood that. But I had grown to love them all by now. Together we had survived Hitler and his vile war, and the very thought that someone might take them from me was my greatest fear. And then, one day, it seemed that this was exactly what was going to happen.

All around Berlin the people of the city were trying to recover, to make life normal once more. And so, as incredible as it might seem in the wake of all that had been, the show-jumping season started up once more at the Sommergarten. In those days I had no horse trailer, but it was not a million miles to reach the ICC, where the grounds of the Sommergarten were located. I walked the horses there, riding Prince and leading Frederick and Arnaud.

I arrived the night before the event and stabled all three of them side by side, which immediately got the other competitors talking. Here was a young girl with three enormous stallions, who were calm and good-natured enough to live cheek by jowl! I was the talk of Sommergarten, which was exactly what I didn't want to be. The last thing I wanted was scrutiny. And soon the talk became dangerous. On the morning of the competition, one of the grooms I'd become friends with, a boy named Franz, came and warned me.

"There's a man looking for you," Franz said. "He says he knows you and your horses."

"What was he like?" I asked Franz.

Franz looked worried. "He was a mean-looking German."

My blood ran cold at this. I had been mad to come here! I had to leave now!

I was in Prince's stable tacking up when there was a scratching noise at the stable door, and then there was the sound of a dog whining with frustration as it tried to get in. I thought of the Nazis with their vicious German shepherds, and I admit I panicked. I was trapped. There was no way out of here.

And then, on the other side of the door, the dog gave

a strangled yelp, and I felt my heart racing, because I knew for sure at that moment that I recognised him. Don't ask me how, but I knew, before I saw him. I just *knew*. And now, instead of being scared, I was tugging at the bolt of the door and scrabbling with my fingers to prise it open, and my heart nearly burst when there he was right in front of me.

"Olaf!"

Have you ever seen a dog when he is truly overjoyed? Olaf behaved like a wild thing! He ran round and round in circles, barking and barking, and then back in the other direction, zig-zagging and howling. He was so excited, and I was laughing at his antics but I was crying at the same time. I had never, ever thought I would see my dog again, and now to have him here, it was like a dream.

"Come here!" I threw my arms round him and hugged him to me and buried my face in the ruff of fur at his neck.

"That is quite the reunion." I heard the clipped German accent, and then the voice behind me added drily, "I can only hope that you are even half as pleased to see me as you are to see him."

"Colonel?" I looked up, scarcely able to believe it. And I found myself wiping my eyes to try and see him clearly, as the tears that were now flowing were ruining my vision.

"Hey, hey, Zofia," the Colonel said kindly, "it's OK, everything is OK."

"I thought you were dead!" I was sobbing now, having given up on stopping the tears. "Hitler told me that the bombs had dropped on Dresden, and I knew you and Olaf were there. I thought you'd died!"

"Hitler told you?" the Colonel was astonished. He was even more astonished when I told him everything – all about the Master and the secret stables of the Reich Chancellery, and the horses I had saved from their death warrant that now lived with me in the Grunewald.

"I have been thinking I should try and take them back to their homes," I said, "but I do not know where to even begin."

"I know," the Colonel said. "I have been doing the same thing. The horses that we managed to save from Dresden wound up along with the others from Hostau in the hands of the American military. Two hundred of the Lipizzaners have made their way back with Alois Podhajsky, the master at the Spanish Riding School in Vienna, but the rest – Lipizzaners and Arabians alike – are to be shipped to the United States."

"So if I return these horses, there is no knowing their fate?"

"I'm afraid so," the Colonel said. "Their best hope of ever making it home one day is to remain for the time being with you."

He looked at Prince, all tacked up. "Are you riding soon?"

"I was running away," I said. "I heard that a German officer was looking for me. But now I know it's you, I will ride."

"Excellent," the Colonel said. "I would love to see how you have progressed. You know I am not here at this competition today by total accident. I've been looking for young talented riders. I'm putting together a show-jumping team – a squad that will be hand-picked by me and taught by my method. Would you be keen to join?"

"Yes, Colonel," I replied.

The Colonel smiled at me. "The war is over now, Zofia. No more ranks and titles. If you like, you may call me Otto."

Later, I would look back on this moment and think about how fortunate I had been to have the chance to be mentored by Otto Müller, not once but twice in my life. For I would join his team and his "method" would take Prince and me to the Olympic Games. And from there we travelled the world, and I became a professional show jumper and spent my whole life doing what I loved.

The Colonel too was true to his word when it came to repatriating the horses. When the Spanish Riding School in Vienna reopened its doors, we made the trip from Berlin to Austria in the horse truck, together with Florian III and Neptune, to deliver them safely home. The owners of the Trakehner and the Selle Français were harder to track down, but eventually we found the families they had been taken from, and they too were returned in tearful reunions.

And that left only Prince. In truth, he belonged to the Janów Estate. And so, with the Colonel at my side for moral support, I returned at last, taking my stallion home.

It was late autumn. Snow had not yet fallen, but there was a bite in the air that made it clear that winter was coming. As we drove through those gates and down the tree-lined driveway, I was swept back to that dark, snowy night when the Master had arrived. So much had happened since then, and yet this place remained, and there were mares and foals in the stables once more.

Prince alighted from the horse float and looked around

and snorted, the way Arabians do, exhaling deep breaths as he took in his surroundings.

"He remembers," I said to the Colonel. "Look at him, he is a colt all over again."

We put Prince back in his same stall, the one where I had hidden beneath the rug that fateful night when the Master came for us, and the Colonel and I went inside to meet the new head of the Janów Estate.

The head of the estate was Polish, like me, and an accomplished and compassionate horseman. He listened carefully as I told him Prince's story, and when I was finished he said, "Thank you for bringing him home, Zofia. You were right to do so. Prince of Poland officially belongs to Janów . . ."

I felt the tears prick my eyes, and I was trembling at the thought of saying goodbye to the horse I loved more than anything in the world. And then the head of Janów said, "And yet he would not be alive today if it were not for your courage, so I think it is only fair to make you a deal, Zofia."

"What kind of deal?" I asked.

"One that will suit us both, I think," he replied. "You may keep Prince, compete him and ride him. But for a month every year, in the spring, you will bring him to us here, so that he may stand at stud over our best mares. In that way, we will keep the bloodlines of Prince of Poland alive and well, and his offspring will be the lifeblood of our stud. But we will never take him from you. He will be your horse, Zofia, now and forever."

\*\*\*

Of course I said yes, Mira. And the bargain was made and kept. For a month every year, Prince would be taken to Janów and in that month his foals were sired, and the Prince of Poland line was established – from Prince to his sons, and then his grandsons and great-grandsons. On those journeys home to Janów, the irony was not lost on me that the Master had stolen Prince so that he could breed the ultimate horse. And, in a way, in the end we did exactly that.

As part of the deal with the estate, I would often take my own mares to Janów as well, and so I had several of Prince's foals sired for myself. Emir was one of those foals, sired by a grandson of Prince. I was there on the night he was born at the stud, and although I had seen hundreds of foals in my time, I knew that this one was going to be special. Everyone knew it. He caused such a fuss at the stud – the grooms all came to look at him because he was such an exquisite beauty. When he stood up for the first time on those long, spindly legs to suckle from his mother, I wept and wept. All I could think was that I was glad he would be safe, that war would not touch him, and neither Hitler nor the Master would ever be able to take him from me. He was the great-grandson of a Prince, and so I named him Emir – "The King".

\*\*\*

Zofia wiped her eyes. "By the time Emir came along, I was old, my bones were too tired for me to ride at competition level the way I once had done. It was frustrating, to say the least, because I knew how great Emir would be in the show-jumping arena. And then you turned up, Mira, the little headstrong, wild thing that you were. So much like me! And I saw the talent in you, the same way that the Colonel had once seen it in me."

The old woman clasped Mira's hands in her own. "You have given me my greatest joy, Mira. To watch you and Emir grow together has meant so very much to me. I was never lucky enough to have grandchildren of my own, but I have you, Mira. You are like a grand-daughter to me, and I shall miss you so very much."

"What do you mean, you'll miss me?" Mira was confused. "I don't understand."

"Mira, you have given Emir his moment to shine. And now both of you are destined for greatness. But greatness will not happen for you in a tiny yard in the Grunewald forest. It's time for you to spread your wings. It was always my dream for you to take Emir and become a Grand Prix partnership. Now you have the chance to live that dream for real. You must take the offer that Princess Jana made you and join Team Unity."

"But I can't do it without you!" Mira was in tears. "I don't want to go."

"You're scared," Zofia said. "I understand that. But I've trained you well. You're ready now to leave me, to find your own path as a rider. And you must think too about Emir. Would you deny him this chance to be a superstar?"

"You want me to take Emir with me? But he's your horse. You love him." Mira was stunned.

"I may be his rightful owner, but he's your horse, Mira," Zofia said. "You have his heart, just as I once had the heart of his great-grandfather. So I am making with you the same bargain I once struck for Prince. For one month, every year, you will bring him home to me. And when springtime comes, there will be new foals in my stables. Little Emirs who look just like him, with coal-black coats that will fade one day to dapple grey and then pure white."

Zofia primped her hair in amusement. "I've turned pure white too, but I do not complain about it! I am grateful to be my age. So many children during the war never got the chance to grow old, so I am blessed. And I have done what I set out to do. My story is told, Mira. Remember it, and take heed of the things around you, because we live in *interesting* times now, still, and your story will make history. It has only just begun . . ."

# The True Story of the Stolen Horses of the Second World War

The events in this book are based on historical fact. In 1939 Hitler annexed Poland, just as Zofia describes in her story. His takeover of Poland to create *Lebensraum* – living space for the Aryan race – would result in the deaths of over five million Polish citizens. The first to be killed were those like Zofia's parents in the story – the intellectuals, priests, teachers and the politicians – those who stood a chance of leading any kind of revolution in response to the Nazi power.

Meanwhile, coming from the other direction into Poland to seize control, was the Russian Red Army. And in the middle of these two terrible adversaries stood the real-life Janów Podlaski Estate, the stud farm with its famous world-class Polish Arabians.

It was the reputation of these elite horses that drew the attention of Gustav Rau, Hitler's Master of Horses. Dr Rau, intent on using his powers during the war to create an equine master race, rescued the Janów stud farm and placed it, along with many others, under German control.

Throughout the war, Hitler's Master of Horses would set about seizing stallions and mares from Europe's best stud farms, with the aim of combining the best blood of the famed Lipizzaners of the Spanish Riding School in Vienna with Polish Arabians, Trakehners and other elite European breeds.

He began his breeding programme for his new 'German' horse at a hidden stud farm in Hostau, Czechoslovakia. Here he branded his horses with their own unique mark – an H with a dagger through it – symbolising the new horses of the Third Reich.

As the Germans began to lose the war, however, the Russian Red Army closed in at Hostau, Janów and Berlin, and the horses were in grave danger. The Red Army's deadly reputation was all too real. When the Hungarians tried to smuggle their own Lipizzaners out to the safety of the Spanish Riding School in Vienna, they were stopped on the roads by the Red Army, who shot the horses on the spot and fed them to their starving troops as dinner.

Meanwhile, in Vienna, the head of the Spanish Riding School, Alois Podhajsky, decided that his famous Haute Ecole Lipizzaner stallions would be safer away from the city as the fighting grew close, so he took them by train to escape the city. They nearly died several times on the journey due to the Allied bombing, but eventually they made it to the safety of the Tyrolean mountain retreat of St Martin. Here they hoped to wait out the war, but as the Germans began to lose on all fronts the Russians, once again, were closing in.

At Janów Estate, too, the Russian threat was close once more. With the end of the war almost upon them, there were soldiers on both sides – German and Americans – who put aside their differences and fought to keep the horses safe. In a series of heroic acts, the two sides worked together to manage a peaceful hand-over of the Janów Estate to the Americans to keep the horses out of Russian hands.

Unfortunately the decision was made that the best way to keep the horses safe would be to flee to Dresden.

This proved to be a terrible mistake, as the bombing of Dresden by the Allies in February 1945 meant that the horses arrived just as the city became a firestorm, and many beautiful stallions perished. The mares and foals, however, had been slower to arrive, and so they survived.

Back in St Martin, Alois Podhajsky, with the help of the horse-loving American General Patton, would rescue 219 of his incredible Lipizzaners and eventually take them home to the Austrian stud farm at Piber.

The Janów Arabians wouldn't return. There was some effort after the war to find their rightful owners. After all, the horses were not dissimilar to the great priceless art, gold and treasure that had been looted by the Nazis, and they should have been returned. But in the end, the horses stolen from Janów and other elite European stables that had survived the war for the most part would not be repatriated. They were officially considered by the Americans to be 'spoils of war', and so 151 priceless Arabians, Lipizzaners and other irreplaceable horses were taken by boat to the United States. Though 151 horses left Germany, 152 arrived in America – one mare had given birth to a foal on the way. These horses were unceremoniously auctioned off to the highest bidders. And so Europe's most elegant purebred Arabians survived the war to end up five thousand miles away, herding cattle on mid-western cow ranches.

Hitler would spend the last 139 days of the war in his bunker and, in the final throes of the war, he flew into fits of rage when he realised that his armies had failed him. To protect Berlin, he resorted to using children as soldiers, including the Hitler Youth and the League of German Girls, the BDM. The girls were not supposed to be involved in armed combat, but there were reports that many took up weapons in the final days. When the Russians drew close to the bunker, Hitler plummeted into utter despair and poisoned his own dogs with cyanide, including his beloved Blondi, rather than let the Russians have them, before killing himself too.

The story of Mira is based on the real modern-day Syrian refugee crisis, and the journey she takes to reach Berlin is a similar route to that taken by many Syrian refugees.

Readers of my earlier books may recognise the fictionalised character of Princess Jana as she is based on the real-life Princess Haya of Jordan from my novel

*The Princess and the Foal.* That story is the recounting of her childhood, and the gift of an orphan foal that would heal the princess's heart following the death of her mother, Queen Alia. The real Princess Haya would go on to represent Jordan as a show jumper in the Olympic Games, become the worldwide president of the FEI and, with the support of her father, the late King Hussein of Jordan, she would establish Team Harmony, the elite international show-jumping squad. Her appearance in this story is an acknowledgement of her inspiring achievements as she continues to be a flag bearer for all young equestriennes with a dream and the will to change our world.

An epic tale of love, loyalty and
the lengths each girl will go to . . .

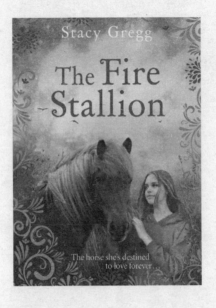

Twelve-year-old Hilly has landed her dream job,
riding on the set of *Brunhilda*, an epic film based
on the fearless warrior of Icelandic legend. Norse
fire ritual tells that on midsummer's day animals
and humans can shapeshift, and one night Hilly
finds herself connected to the young warrior and
her fire stallion . . .

One girl's refusal to give up, even in the face
of impossible odds . . .

When an earthquake hits Parnassus on New Zealand's
South Island, Evie and the rest of the town are forced
to evacuate. But when she realises that she'll be forced
to leave her pony, Gus, behind, Evie refuses to join the
others and abandon her best friend . . .

Every girl dreams of becoming a princess.
But this real-life princess has a dream of her own.

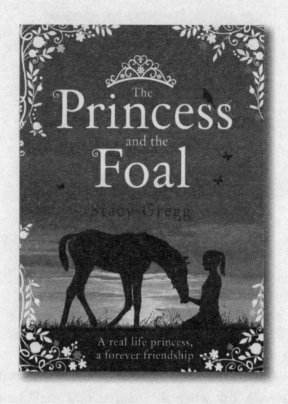

Discover the incredible story
of Princess Haya and her foal.

Two girls divided by time, united by their love
for some very special horses, in this epic
Caribbean adventure.

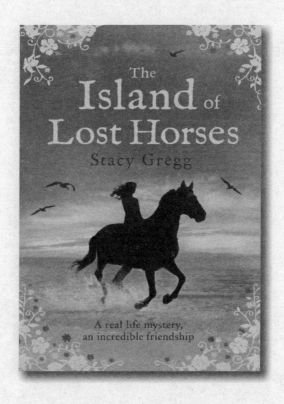

Based on the extraordinary true story of the
Abaco Barb, a real-life mystery that has
remained unsolved for over five hundred years.

An epic story of two girls and their bond
with beloved horses, sweeping between Italy
during the Second World War and the present day.

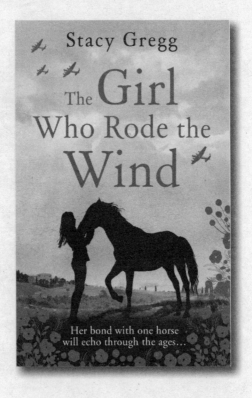

One family's history of adventure and
heartbreak – and how it is tied to the world's
most dangerous horse race, the Palio.